MAGICAL B

NORTHERN SOUL

Happy reading!

Liz Hedgecock

LIZ HEDGECOCK

WHITE
RHINO
BOOKS

For Enriqueta Rylands (1843-1908)
without whom there would be no
John Rylands Library

CHAPTER 1

A buzz came from Luke's phone, magnified by the bookshop's wooden counter to the level of an angry wasp.

He glanced at it: Ben, the bookshop manager, had sent a text. As he was in the middle of serving a customer, he ignored it.

'Good book you have there,' he said to the customer, a sandy-haired woman of indeterminate age, who had put a copy of *The Impossible Thing* on the counter.

'Have you read it?' she asked.

He grinned. 'One of the perks of working in Burns Books. Though you have to be quick, because the best books don't hang around. I'm amazed we've got a copy of this already: it hasn't been out that long.'

The phone buzzed again.

'Cash or card?' said Luke. 'Would you like a bag?'

'Oh no, I have one here,' she said. 'Got to save the planet and all that.'

'Oh yes, absolutely.'

The woman touched the card to the reader and a receipt

1

spooled out. 'Do come back and tell me what you think of it,' said Luke, with a smile.

'Oh, I shall,' she said, enthusiastically. Em looked over from the café counter and smirked at him. 'Bye for now.'

'Luke.' Ben had actually left his position at the ground-floor till and was standing at the foot of the stairs. 'I texted you.'

'I was serving a customer,' said Luke.

'Yes, he was,' said the woman, holding up her tote bag.

'Did you bother to read the message I sent you?'

The customer raised her eyebrows, skirted round Ben and went upstairs.

Luke eyed his phone. *Can you come up pls.*

'I can,' he said. 'Although it might be a bit tricky.'

'Tricky or not, make it happen,' said Ben. 'Jemma's asked me to pop to the Friendly Bookshop ASAP. It sounds important, so I need to be there soonest. Can't keep the big boss waiting.'

One of the many things Luke disliked about Ben was his use of words such as *ASAP*, *soonest* and *the big boss*. 'My lunch break is in' – he checked his watch – 'five minutes.'

Ben rolled his eyes. 'I'll make it quick. Don't worry, you'll get your lunch.'

'Will it be soon enough?' As no customers were present, Luke grinned and ran his tongue over his long, sharp canines. 'My breaks do have to be *very* regular, or I can't answer for the consequences. So you really should be back ASAP.'

'Fine,' said Ben. 'Now get upstairs, will you.' His

2

footsteps thundered in that direction, followed by the loud bang of the front door.

Luke stroked the shop counter, which was slightly warmer than usual and had begun to pulse. 'It isn't your fault,' he said. 'Just Ben being Ben.'

'The shop knows,' said Em, with a resigned smile. 'Go on, get yourself on the upstairs till. If you can't hold out any longer, text me and I'll hold the fort while you eat.'

'Thanks.' Luke headed upstairs.

The counter was littered with books and paper and ornamented with Folio, the original bookshop cat, who had wandered over from his usual home at The Friendly Bookshop. He was reclining on a large sheet of paper which appeared blank. When he stood and stretched in response to Luke's caress, Luke saw that the paper was headed *IDEAS* in Ben's blocky capitals. He snorted, and squared up the papers.

Between serving customers, he shelved the non-fiction books and alphabetised the novels to go downstairs. *I wonder why Jemma wants Ben*, he thought.

Another reason for his dislike of Ben was that Ben held the prestigious role of Assistant Keeper for Westminster and was therefore a member of the Keepers' Guild. In Luke's opinion, he was entirely unworthy. Not that he could do anything: Ben had been recruited fair and square (well, squareish) by a then-senior member of the Guild. And while Luke was confident that Ben wouldn't know how to handle a book emergency if one took place under his nose, the role was permanent.

She's probably telling him about something cool right

now, he thought. *They'll go to Rolando's for a coffee and a pastry, Ben will order the biggest, stickiest one there is, then ignore what Jemma's saying while he eats it. In the meantime, I'm doing his job and starving to death.* He cast a longing look towards the back room, where his lunch was waiting in the fridge and no doubt maturing nicely.

Oh, do get over yourself. That thought seemed to be in Maddy's voice. *You'll get a break on your honeymoon.*

Maddy, his fiancée, worked at The Friendly Bookshop and spent her time outside work (and some when the shop was quiet) organising their Gothic-themed wedding. The plan was to book it as soon as Luke had obtained the necessary documents.

When Luke was born, birth certificates hadn't been invented. Even if they had, a centuries-old bridegroom was bound to raise a few eyebrows. In appearance he was permanently stuck at twenty-five, the age when he had become a vampire. However, as the staff of Burns Books and The Friendly Bookshop had cause to know, appearances could be deceptive.

Luke spent the next twenty minutes of comparative tranquility hoping Jemma had found Ben a stupendously boring task that had to be done away from both shops. He was rewarded when Ben returned with a face like thunder and said 'Take a break, then.'

Luke thought about asking for a thank you, decided lunch was more important and headed first for the kitchen and then to the stockroom, where he could eat in privacy if he locked the door.

Five minutes later, he rinsed the Tupperware container

4

in the kitchen, then went to wash his hands and face and brush his teeth, just in case. That done, he went back to the stockroom to pick up a couple of boxes of books for downstairs.

The stockroom of Burns Books had an interesting quirk, which was that however you tried to organise it, the shop had other ideas. You could pack a box full of romance novels, and in the time it took to take it to the vaulted basement, they would become a box of cozy mysteries. Luke chose to think that the shop knew what was needed, while Ben regarded it as rampant disobedience. Not that he could do a thing about it.

'Have you had your break?' Em asked, as soon as he arrived downstairs with the first box.

'I have, no thanks to Ben. For all he knows, I might have made plans with Maddy.'

'Had you?'

'That's not the point. I might have.' He went upstairs for the other box. Usually he and Maddy did eat lunch together, but lately Maddy had been so focused on the wedding that he'd taken to reading or watching something on his phone in the stockroom instead.

Once he brought down the novels from the upstairs counter, which had mercifully stayed in order, Luke attempted to begin shelving. He'd chosen a box of thrillers and one of literary fiction from the stockroom, on the grounds that that was what they'd sold most of that morning. The thriller box had made it downstairs without any tampering on the shop's behalf, but when he opened the box of literary fiction, he found a book called *Ace Your*

5

Interview sitting on top.

Luke lifted it out. Immediately, Folio jumped on the counter and rubbed his head against it.

'I'm glad you approve,' said Luke.

The next book in the box was *The Million-Dollar Answer: How To Wow When The Focus Is On You.* 'What the heck…'

Em looked over. 'What's up?'

'The shop's done a switcheroo. I wanted literary fiction, and it's given me…' He pulled out a few more books. 'Books about getting a new job.' He frowned. 'Should I be worried? I mean, Ben isn't my biggest fan, not by a long way, and he's just come back from a meeting with Jemma.'

'Which she invited him to,' said Em. 'Anyway, if Ben was planning to fire you, not that he can, the shop would probably present you with books on budget meals and making a fortune as an eBay reseller. It's nothing if not practical. I'm not saying you couldn't get another job, but…'

But jobs suitable for vampires are few and far between. 'I hope you're right,' said Luke. 'In the meantime, these need shelving upstairs with the non-fiction.'

Em checked her watch. 'My break officially starts in ten minutes, but as it's quiet I might head up early. I may even find time for a chat with Ben.'

'You're a star.'

One of Luke's most useful skills was his ability to cast glamour. It was fairly normal for a vampire, and very handy in his customer-facing role at Burns Books. It had also been useful when he'd accompanied Jemma on

6

various bookish expeditions, particularly in winning over wary librarians or members of the public. He had also given Em tuition, though she had considerable natural charm of her own. Unlike Luke's glamour, hers worked a treat on Ben.

'If there's anything worth knowing, I'll fill you in later,' said Em. She collected her denim jacket and shoulder bag from the coat rack and sauntered upstairs.

Luke concentrated on listening – his hearing was, unsurprisingly, batlike in its clarity when he chose. Sure enough, Em purred 'Hello, Ben.'

'Oh, hi, Em.' Ben's tone was markedly softer. It was no secret that Em had been going out with Damon for years, but hope springs eternal. 'Are you going on your break?'

'I will in a minute. Oh, silly me. I meant to bring a box of books upstairs for you, but I forgot.'

'I'll get them now, if you don't mind waiting.'

Thirty seconds and a stampede downstairs later, Ben came into view.

Luke pointed silently at the box. Ben hefted it, then set off as if he was in second place in the Highland Games. Luke shook his head at the rapidly retreating back.

A short man in an appropriately autumnal jumper accosted him for help. 'I'm trying to read the Jack Parlabane books in order. Do you have any?'

'Oh yes,' said Luke. 'Can you remember which one you read last?'

'Let me think. There was definitely a murder…'

Luke suppressed a sigh, then realised there was a better way. 'Tell you what, I've just got a box of thrillers from the stockroom. Why don't you have a quick look in there?'

'I could try…' He opened the box. 'Well I never! What are the chances of that?' He pulled out *Attack of the Unsinkable Rubber Ducks* and stared at it. Then he checked inside the cover. 'It is the next one! How remarkable…' He put it on the counter. 'Oh, and I'd like a £25 gift card for my niece.'

For the next forty minutes or so, Luke was kept occupied by a steady trickle of customers. Occasionally he had room to wonder what, if anything, Em had managed to winkle out of Ben, but before he could begin speculating, another customer would claim his attention, or he would need to neaten the shelves after a particularly enthusiastic rummage.

That said, by the time Em reappeared for the run-up to afternoon tea, Luke felt distinctly jumpy. 'Come on,' he said. 'Tell me: I can take it. Should I have an espresso first?'

Em laughed. 'You're already a bag of nerves, Luke. The last thing you need is coffee. I'll make you a decaf tea.'

A few minutes later she brought it to the counter, with a shortbread biscuit in the saucer and an espresso shot for herself.

'Thank you,' said Luke, and took a long sip. 'Well…?'

Em leaned in, and for a second Luke wondered if she was planning to use her charm on him, though for the life of him he couldn't think why. 'Don't worry, you still have a job,' she murmured.

Luke exhaled and his shoulders relaxed. 'Thank heavens for that.'

'I haven't finished,' whispered Em. 'Ben still has a job.'

'I thought you told me not to worry.'

Em held up a finger. 'Not the job he had when he went to see Jemma. He's asked for a transfer into a non-Keeper role, outside the Guild. Apparently she asked him to sort out a book emergency for her and he felt he wasn't ready. That he'll never be ready. So . . . she'll be recruiting.'

'Oh really?' said Luke. He had a terrible urge to rub his hands and cackle like a villain, but decided it was bad form. Besides, the impossible thing had happened: he actually felt sorry for Ben.

CHAPTER 2

Luke's text came at half past four: *Fancy a drink after work? x*

Maddy considered. She wasn't a huge fan of after-work drinks: she didn't really have a head for alcohol and a packet of crisps wasn't enough to stop her feeling slightly woozy. In addition, she was eating salad for lunch most days at the moment, since she aimed to be suitably slender to do justice to a Gothic wedding dress.

She frowned at the phone. Another factor to take into account was that Luke would almost certainly want to go to the Rat and Compasses, a shabby dive to which he was inexplicably attached. If they went there, she would probably end up with a slimline tonic: the bar staff wouldn't know a mocktail if it stole the dried-out lemon slices from under their noses.

But that wasn't all. She had been serving on the counter of the Friendly Bookshop when Ben swaggered in. 'I have a meeting with Jemma,' he said, looking past Maddy for the object of his interest.

'She's working from home today,' said Maddy. 'I'll text her to let her know you've arrived.' It felt ridiculous to send a text to someone who was sitting above her head, but it was considerably more decorous than going to the foot of the stairs and bellowing.

She picked up her phone and scrolled to Jemma's number. *Ben's here for a meeting*, she typed.

Thanks, I'll come down.

Maddy liked to think that Jemma's trust in her was growing. Most days now, she left Maddy to open the shop, and she was encouraging her to make more of the day-to-day decisions, such as how to dress the window and what sort of stock they needed. Jemma had even suggested that Maddy take Gertrude the ancient orange VW camper van on book-hunting expeditions. Gertrude actually belonged to Raphael, eccentric owner of Burns Books and former head of the Keepers' Guild in England, but she was always available for bookish jaunts. However, having ridden in Gertrude more than once and experienced her little ways, Maddy had politely declined.

A few minutes later, Jemma appeared, in her usual black trousers teamed with an unusually floaty floral top. 'Hello, Ben. Thanks for coming over.'

'Oh, I like your top,' said Maddy. 'That really suits you.'

'Thank you!' Jemma beamed. The top did suit her: her reddish-brown hair shone and her skin glowed. Maddy was relieved: there had been a few mornings lately where Jemma had come downstairs looking haggard. Maddy had put it down to nightmares about the trauma from a few months previously, when everything had seemed on the point of destruction.

Jemma turned to Ben. 'Shall we go to Rolando's? My treat.'

'Don't mind if I do,' said Ben, with a distinct smirk.

Men, thought Maddy. *Always ruled by their appetite.*

Jemma returned less than half an hour later, distinctly less serene.

'What did you do with Ben?' Maddy asked.

'Oh, he's gone back to Burns Books to sulk,' said Jemma. 'Which is just what I need right now. Here.' She put a paper bag on the counter. 'I got you a cinnamon roll.'

'Oh, thank you!'

'No problem. If you're not busy, could you send me a link to the Assistant Keeper folder? You'll find it in HR. Thanks: time for me to make a few phone calls.' And Jemma headed upstairs before Maddy had a chance to reply.

So, she thought, opening the shop's laptop and clicking through the files. *A vacancy, from the look of things.*

When Luke's text arrived, she was only surprised that it had taken him so long. Hopefully that meant he was at best reluctant or at least unsure about applying for Ben's post.

She decided to give him the benefit of the doubt. *Yes, why not. Can we go to the Ship and Shovell?*

The Rat and Compasses is more private. Pick you up at 5.30?

OK

Maddy put her phone down, sighed, and as the shop was quiet, did a search on winter table centrepieces. *A mix*

12

of crimson and deep violet roses would be nice.

***

Luke returned from the bar with a Bloody Mary and a slimline tonic with ice, no lemon. 'I suppose you're wondering what the occasion is.'

Maddy considered letting him off the hook, but why should she? 'We don't need an occasion to go out for a drink after work, do we?'

'Mmm.' Luke stirred his drink with the paper straw. 'How would you feel about me applying for a new job?'

So much for reluctance. 'What, now?' said Maddy. 'With our wedding coming up?'

'Yes, but you're organising most of that. I've been sorting my documents. Hopefully they'll arrive soon and then it's just suit shopping.'

'Haven't we had enough excitement over the last year? That's how long you've been at Burns Books, more or less. Can't we enjoy the peace and quiet for a bit before you go looking for another opportunity?'

'I wouldn't have to leave,' said Luke. 'That's the cool thing. Ben's job is up for grabs. Maybe we could even do a straight swap. That would be really efficient.'

A series of images flashed through Maddy's mind. Her first encounter with Luke; helping him transform into a colony of bats and back again; realising her mind was being controlled by her old boss; resigning from her job with everyone else to support Jemma, who was on the run from the police. 'I don't want you to,' she said, instead of all that.

'Why not? It'll be exciting.'

'For you, maybe. Going off to deal with book emergencies, while I wait in the shop wondering whether you'll ever return.'

'Aren't you being a bit dramatic?'

'No.' Maddy took a gulp of her tonic water to relieve her dry mouth and slammed the glass on the table. Then she sighed. 'I'd just like a quiet life for a few months. Is that so much to ask?'

'I might never get the chance again.' Luke looked utterly woebegone, and in his pale-green eyes she saw the little boy he must have been hundreds of years ago.

She put her hand on his and interlaced her fingers with his long pale ones. 'Of course you will. Jemma thinks highly of you, and so does Raphael. The fact that Ben can't stand you is probably a point in your favour.'

That made him giggle. 'You must admit, it would be convenient.'

'Maybe I value peace of mind more than convenience,' said Maddy.

Luke sipped his Bloody Mary, still gazing at her. 'Do you really?' He put the glass down. 'The setup you've got is pretty convenient.'

'So is yours,' said Maddy.

'But I want more! I don't want to just sell books, I want to protect them! To look after them. And when I say look after them, I don't mean unfolding the dog ears and shelving them nicely. Can't you understand that?'

Maddy grabbed a beermat and picked at its edge. 'I've always wanted a job that revolved around books, either in a library or a bookshop. I chose Brian's bookshop because it had special books, *prized* books. I appreciate the acquisition and the preservation of knowledge, of course I do. That doesn't mean I want to run round libraries subduing unruly books like some sort of dog trainer. I prefer my books calm and well behaved. Is that so wrong?'

'Not at all,' said Luke. 'I don't think it's just that. It's the magic part too, isn't it?'

'It's mostly the danger,' said Maddy. But Luke had hit a nerve. She'd been subject to other people's magic too many times to approve of it. The thought of Luke being encouraged to sharpen his already considerable skills was more than she could bear, even if it kept him safe from harm.

'I wish you could understand.'

'I do,' said Maddy. 'It just isn't in me.' She squeezed his hand. 'Look, I can't stop you applying and I wouldn't anyway. It's your decision. I *can* tell you that I don't want you to apply. I worry about you anyway, without adding more to fret over.'

'Maybe you worry too much.' Luke gently withdrew his hand and finished his drink.

'Back to mine? *Interview With The Vampire* is on tonight.' Luke came to hers most nights. His studio flat was tiny and dark, and the bed, such as it was, most uncomfortable. She hoped he'd give it up once they were married.

'I might go for a walk,' said Luke. 'A long walk.'

She knew what that meant. There was a slight flush in his cheeks, and his eyes shone in the way they often did when he'd helped with a book emergency or they'd had a

15

row. Excitement or strong emotion released adrenaline, and as a non-practising vampire, Luke's outlets were limited. She couldn't blame him: he was only inhuman.

She could see him in her mind's eye: strolling in the London streets until they were dark and quiet, then making his way to Trafalgar Square, waiting for a pigeon to approach, and... She shivered.

'I promise I'll be careful,' said Luke. 'I'll text you when I get back. Or I could stop by, if it's not too late.'

'A text will be fine,' said Maddy, quickly. The thought of Luke snuggling up, after gorging on the blood of a more or less defenceless pigeon... 'Maybe we can discuss the job thing tomorrow, once you've slept on it.'

'Yeah, maybe,' said Luke, and she knew his mind was already made up. 'I'll try and catch Jemma tomorrow, see what she thinks.'

Luke walked her home before he set off. Maddy watched him stride away, his long black coat flapping behind him. *If I'd known what I was getting involved with...* She shook herself. *I wouldn't want him any different.*

Or would I?

Maddy let herself into her flat, double-locked the door, bolted it, then went into the sitting room and drew the curtains. *Ridiculous that I'm engaged to a vampire and terrified of burglars.*

She went to the kitchen and inspected the fridge. She took out a pack of tofu and a bag of stir-fry veg, and tried not to think about what Luke was planning to have for his tea. *He's mostly vegan*, she thought. *It's an occasional lapse. He can't help it.*

If he gets that job, with all the excitement, how many lapses will there be?

And how long will it be until he gets tired of me?

I just want a quiet, peaceful life with the man of my dreams, she thought, as she sliced the tofu into cubes with uncharacteristic viciousness. *Even if my dreams are someone else's nightmares.*

CHAPTER 3

Luke woke with a deep sense of shame and a coppery tang in his mouth, though he'd brushed his teeth thoroughly when he got home. After he'd texted Maddy that he was back safe, of course. The taste was an innate memory.

He rolled over and groped for his phone in the dark. *6.30.* His alarm wouldn't ring till seven o'clock, but he felt fully rested. Sated, even. *Ugh.*

He climbed out of his narrow bed, which really was only made for one person, with its wooden sides. Not precisely a coffin, but with the same sense of enclosure.

Why did I… Then he remembered, and sat up. *What shall I wear?*

He turned the bed into a sofa by the simple expedient of lowering the lid and plonking the pillows on top, then padded to the kitchenette and switched the kettle on. While he normally drank decaf, sometimes a strong black coffee was required.

Once he had a bitter, scalding brew in hand, he wandered to the clothes rail in the corner.

What should an aspiring Assistant Keeper wear? Ben, the latest incumbent of the role, generally rocked up in a suit, or a blazer, polo shirt and chinos if he was feeling casual. Then again, he was as much use as a chocolate teapot.

Luke had seen glimpses of other Assistant Keepers via Jemma's laptop, if she was running a Zoom meeting in the bookshop, but that just showed head and shoulders, and the only common sartorial note was mild eccentricity. Lennox Nash, who had briefly deputised for Raphael as Keeper for England back in the day, had been exceptionally well dressed, and now he was in prison awaiting trial for his part in an attempted coup. Jemma favoured smartish casual, while her former boss Raphael seemed to have made it his personal mission to wear garments that clashed.

In the end Luke selected his favourite black trousers, which accentuated his slim hips, and a loose pale-green shirt which more or less matched his eyes. Anything else was trying too hard. The decision made, he headed for the minuscule bathroom and turned on the shower.

When he emerged, dripping and gasping, his phone screen was bright. A text from Maddy. *Hope today goes well x*

Thank you, he replied. *I'll let you know x*

Despite taking his time, he was at Burns Books by quarter past eight. The shop was dark and silent: he expected nothing less. As the senior member of staff based there, Ben was nominally the keyholder, but he usually strode in at nine-fifteen or later, cheerfully blaming a hold-up on the tube or a gridlock on one of the bridges.

Luke pulled out the key, which he wore on a chain round his neck, and opened the door. When he'd first begun working there, he had been surprised that the bookshop wasn't fitted with an alarm. Later, he realised that any burglar who tried to mess with the shop would come to the stickiest of ends when they least expected it.

He put on the lights and began getting ready for the day. The shop was in good order, which suggested it thoroughly approved of Ben's decision. Luke ran a caressing hand over the mahogany counter. 'I should think so too,' he murmured.

As he was putting his lunch in the fridge, he heard a pronounced squeak from the door which led upstairs to Raphael's flat.

A minute later Raphael wandered in, his tall thin frame resplendent in a silk dressing gown which combined paisley and fractals. Not for the first time, Luke wondered where Raphael shopped for clothes, or if he somehow magicked them up.

'Morning,' said Raphael, and yawned. 'I believe changes are afoot.'

Of course he would know. Raphael Burns, as Keeper Emeritus, was still very much part of both Burns Books and the Keepers' Guild.

'What do you think?' Luke asked, as casually as he could bear.

'You're looking smart today,' Raphael observed. 'If you'd like my personal opinion, I feel that borrowing a couple of Earl Grey teabags for a morning brew will improve my mood immensely.' He filched a couple from the caddy and beamed at Luke.

'I meant—'

'While I am nominally the proprietor of Burns Books, I tend to favour a hands-off approach these days. Perhaps we should wait and see.'

'Yes,' said Luke. He flicked the kettle on, then spooned decaf coffee into a mug. He was already a bag of nerves and he hadn't even made contact with Jemma.

He left that until nine thirty, which seemed timely but not hasty. At that point he fled to the stockroom, locked the door, and spent ten minutes typing, deleting, retyping, swearing under his breath and scowling whenever anyone walked past the door.

Hi Jemma, could we have a chat today if you're not too busy? He pressed *Send* before he could second-guess himself, shoved the phone in his pocket and chose a box of books at random for an alibi.

His pocket buzzed as he was taking the box downstairs. He put the box behind the counter and retrieved his phone.

Sure, we can take a quick walk at lunchtime. Call for me at 12.30?

That's great, thanks, he replied.

Three hours to go, he thought, and went to tidy the shelves, his go-to activity when he needed busywork to keep him occupied.

'Aren't you going to unpack that box?' said Em.

'Maybe later,' Luke replied. In truth, he didn't want to know what was inside. The shop, though helpful to those who treated it well, could be brutally honest. If he opened it and found books called *When Hell Freezes Over* or *Fat Chance, Loser*, he'd chicken out. He knew he would.

***

At quarter past twelve, Luke closed the basement till and headed upstairs.

'Where do you think you're going?' said Ben.

'Business meeting,' said Luke. 'With Jemma.' He was through the door before Ben had a chance to object. Luckily, the day was gloomy, making sunglasses optional rather than a necessity.

Jemma was standing outside The Friendly Bookshop when he arrived. 'Sorry, am I late?' he asked.

'No, I'm early,' said Jemma. 'I fancied some fresh air. Well, as fresh as you can get in London. Shall we head for the Phoenix Garden?'

'Why not?' Luke felt slightly put out that he wouldn't get a pastry and a coffee, but hopefully the change of venue was auspicious.

'Come on, then.'

They walked briskly down Charing Cross Road, slowing occasionally to check out other bookshops' window displays. It was a short walk to the garden, and a few minutes later they sat on a bench together, gazing at a pond buzzing with busy insects and bordered by tall reeds. It reminded Luke of London.

'So, what do you want to chat about?' Jemma asked.

He turned to her and slung an arm over the back of the bench. 'I heard on the grapevine that Ben's giving up the Assistant Keeper role.'

'News travels fast,' said Jemma. He waited for her to

say more, but she didn't.

'I was wondering...' After a minute or so, Jemma raised her eyebrows. 'I was wondering if I should apply.'

'I see,' said Jemma.

'I know I won't have as much experience as the other candidates, but I'm willing to learn, and I could study in my spare time, and...' The sympathy in her face silenced him.

'The thing is, Luke... You've experienced at first hand what happens when someone who isn't ready gets put in a senior role.' She leaned towards him. 'Between you and me, when I asked Ben to attend a knowledge emergency yesterday, I knew he wouldn't go.'

'I'd do a better job than Ben, I can promise you that.'

'You would,' Jemma said quietly. 'One day you'll make a great Assistant Keeper. But not yet. And I don't want you to get hurt in the process of trying.'

Luke remained silent. He had a lump forming in his throat, and a horrible feeling that if he tried to speak it would come out as if he was on the verge of tears. Which he wasn't.

'After I spoke to Ben yesterday, I reflected on our recruitment process,' said Jemma. 'To be frank, it isn't rigorous enough. So when I recruit to the Assistant Keeper role in Westminster, I'll pilot an assessment centre.'

'That sounds painful. What does it actually mean?'

Jemma smiled. 'I'm sorry: management jargon. Instead of the current process, which is an application form plus panel interview, I'm thinking of introducing two extra elements. So there'll be an application form, an interview, a brief written test, and finally a practical. A solo practical.'

Luke's heart sank. Jemma was absolutely right. He'd accompanied her to a few low-level knowledge emergencies, and occasionally captured an errant book himself under supervision, but he'd never gone out alone. Neither would he want to, yet.

Then he thought of something. 'Hang on a minute. *You* learned on the job.'

Jemma pondered for a moment, watching a dragonfly hover above the surface of the pond. 'Yes, I did, mostly,' she said. 'It wasn't ideal. I ended up in several situations where I had no idea what I was doing and I had to trust to a combination of luck and my own powers. Powers which sometimes I didn't know I had. I could have been hurt. I could have died, even. I don't want that to happen to anyone I have responsibility for.' She shot him a look. 'Sorry to get all serious, but it's important that you know what you'd be getting into.'

Luke sighed. 'I understand. I'm disappointed, but I get it.'

'I knew you would.' Jemma held out a hand. Luke took it and they shook hands solemnly. Jemma gave his hand an extra squeeze before she released it. 'To be honest, Luke, I'm seeking people who are already Assistant Keepers and wish to move to a more demanding patch.' She paused. 'I hope you don't mind, but I have a couple of favours to ask.'

'Go on.'

'First, would you help me run the assessment centre? You'll keep a cool head, and observing the process could help you identify development areas for the future.'

Luke grinned at Jemma's management speak. 'OK. What's the other favour?'

'Well,' said Jemma, shifting slightly towards him on the bench. 'Something's come up in another region. A minor matter, but it would really help you to build your experience in dealing with low-level book misbehaviour.'

Luke's eyes lit up and he slid along the bench until they were almost touching. His pulse quickened. 'Tell me more.'

CHAPTER 4

'It's in Manchester.'

'*Manchester?* You said it was in a different region, but…' Luke tried to remember what he knew of Manchester. He'd never been, that was for sure. Manchester had barely existed when he was getting his education, or not as far as he was concerned. He had a vague idea of cotton mills, railways and clanking machinery. Oh, and Liam Gallagher, though he doubted he'd be involved.

'It isn't that far,' said Jemma. 'Two hours on the train from Euston. And it's usually overcast, so you won't have to worry about too much light. I visited when I was choosing which universities to apply for. It's a lovely city – lots going on – but my mum put her foot down. She said it was too far away.'

Exactly, thought Luke, pushing down the panic rising within him. 'So… What would you want me to do?'

Jemma sat back and crossed her legs. 'To be honest, I'm not entirely sure. I haven't had a request for help as such, and there haven't been any reports of book-related incidents.'

'So what's the problem? Why are you interested?'

Jemma looked thoughtful. 'This probably sounds like something and nothing, but I belong to several groups on Facebook that focus on bookshops and libraries. You know the sort of thing – they share memes, book quizzes, photos of libraries and books they've bought, and so on. Comforting, cosy, low-stakes stuff.'

'Yeeees…' Luke had a nodding acquaintance with Facebook in that he occasionally posted on the shops' social-media accounts, usually photos of books or cats. Maddy tended to spend more time on Pinterest and Instagram, apart from an Ann Radcliffe fan group he found slightly weird. Anyway, Facebook unnerved him. People could present themselves as anything, and you'd never know the truth. Plus, he obviously couldn't present his whole self, not if he wanted a quiet life. What was *he* supposed to do? He shook off the frustration and suspicion stealing over him. 'Go on, Jemma.'

'A fortnight or so ago, I saw a post where someone said they'd had a bit of a funny turn in the John Rylands Library, which is in Manchester. I didn't think anything of it at the time: I just thought they'd stood up too quickly or drunk too much coffee. Then I read another post about the library by someone else, in a different group. It wasn't anything definitive – no flying books, smashed windows or weird smells – but I wondered.'

'So what did they say happened?'

'The second person said they were in the reading room

and when they walked past the statue of Enriqueta Rylands, they suddenly felt cold and shivery. As if someone was walking over their grave, they said. Or as if they were walking over someone's grave.' She shrugged. 'One of the two.'

'What did the first person say?'

'You wouldn't believe how long it took me to find their post,' Jemma said conversationally. 'I thought it was in the same Facebook group, but it wasn't, so I ended up trawling through ten or fifteen groups to find it. It didn't help that I was upstairs in the flat and the kittens were climbing on me.'

'So, the post…' Luke prompted. *Is there such a thing as a shaggy-cat story?*

'Sorry. Eventually I found it, and the person said they'd been on their own in the reading room just before closing. When they headed for the main door, they said it was like wading through mud. The closer they got to the door, the harder it became to move: something was pulling them back. Apparently, their head was spinning and they felt as if they were sinking into the floor. Luckily, someone came in, saw them and got them to a chair in one of the study areas. And the person said that as soon as the other person touched them, it was as if a spell had been lifted.'

'Mmm.' Luke grinned. 'Are you sure that isn't the normal magic of libraries and bookshops? I never want to leave one once I'm inside. Not as long as it's behaving itself, of course.'

'I take your point,' said Jemma. 'But two incidents, even minor ones, in the same room of the same library in the space of a week seems a bit odd to me.'

'Have you spoken to the Assistant Keeper up there?'

'I've tried,' said Jemma. 'Since I started this role, I've been aiming to speak to every Assistant Keeper individually at least once a quarter, to check that everything's going well. I've never managed to speak to Ludovic, the Assistant Keeper for Manchester, for more than two minutes at a time.'

'Doesn't that worry you?'

Jemma considered. 'Not really: he's very busy. I mean, there's the John Rylands, Central Library, the Portico, Chetham's, the university libraries, plus all the libraries and bookshops in Greater Manchester. It's a ridiculously big workload.' She mused for a moment. 'I should probably divide it somehow, or suggest we recruit junior Keepers to spread the load – *that* would be an innovation – but Ludovic may not like that.'

'How do you know, if you've barely spoken to him?' said Luke.

'There is that. Maybe I should send him an email.'

'About splitting Manchester, or about the incidents?'

'Probably the first,' said Jemma, after a while. 'I'm not sure I want to bother him with something that could be a coincidence.'

Luke raised his eyebrows. 'So why are you sending me all the way up there to investigate?'

'I don't want to send you away, Luke,' said Jemma. 'But it's not convenient to go myself, it may be useful to you, and frankly, I'm not sure who else to ask.'

'Surely you have staff or other contacts who live closer

and are experienced investigators.'

'That's the thing,' said Jemma. 'I'm not looking to you to conduct an investigation as such. I don't want you prowling round the reading room in a mask and gauntlets, then interviewing the library staff and writing in a little notebook.'

'You make me sound like a cross between Van Helsing and Miss Marple,' said Luke.

Jemma's smile was rather shamefaced. 'Sorry, it wasn't intentional. What I'd be asking you to do is travel to the library and have a wander around the reading room, since that's where things are happening. See if you pick up any vibes, maybe have a casual chat with the staff, observe what other visitors are doing…'

'So it isn't an opportunity to hone my skills and make me Assistant Keeper-ready,' said Luke, flatly. 'It's several hours stuck on a train to spend an hour or so in a library and *pick up vibes*. That's a complete waste of time and money.'

Jemma looked hurt. 'Don't be like that, Luke.'

'Well, it is. It would make much more sense to monitor social media and see if anything else comes up about this library. Or to contact the people who posted and get more information from them. Or to email this Ludovic guy and get him on the case. It's on his patch. I don't have time to go on a wild-goose chase, what with the wedding to plan.'

'I thought Maddy was taking the lead on that,' said Jemma.

'I'm doing stuff too! Besides, I'll be busy keeping Burns Books running. Now Ben's stepped down, he'll probably do even less than his usual bare minimum.'

'OK,' said Jemma, seeming small and defeated, and Luke felt suddenly guilty. 'I know recruiting Ben's replacement has to be my priority.' She regarded him rather sadly. 'Do you still want to be involved in running the assessment centre?'

'Yes. That makes sense.' He was about to say *Unlike this Manchester nonsense*, but stopped himself just in time. His eyebrows drew together. *Am I overreacting?* He wasn't even sure why he was so hostile to the idea of going to Manchester. Most people would be perfectly happy to go on a free work jolly, particularly one where Ben wasn't invited.

'Good.' Jemma sighed, and got up slowly from the bench. 'I'll get an internal advert out for the Assistant Keeper role and start planning the assessment centre. As for Manchester, I guess I'll have to go to Plan B.'

'What's Plan B?'

Jemma shrugged. 'Dunno.'

That made Luke feel guilty again. But honestly – going all the way to Manchester in search of *vibes*? For what was perhaps the first time, he found himself questioning his boss's judgement.

'Come on, we'd better get back. You'll want your lunch.' Jemma gave him a weak smile, and another pang shot through him.

But he held firm. *Whatever Plan B is, it won't involve me, that's for sure*, he thought. *Maddy gets nervous if I so much as go for a walk at night. If I tell her I'm heading to Manchester, she'll throw a fit. Especially just before our*

31

wedding. And as he walked to Burns Books, he felt confident that he had done the right thing in refusing Jemma's daft request.

CHAPTER 5

'…so if you could recommend one?'

Maddy regarded the customer blankly. 'I'm so sorry, I didn't catch what you said.'

'Which is the best Jane Austen novel to start with, if you haven't read any before?' The customer was a wisp of a woman who appeared in her sixties at least. Maddy wondered how on earth she had managed not to read an Austen novel in her life so far.

'Oh.' Maddy considered. '*Northanger Abbey* is my favourite, but lots of people go for *Pride and Prejudice* because that's the one everyone's heard of. We almost always have a copy in stock. It'll be near the beginning of the novel section, over there.' She pointed. 'Or… If you read it and decide you're all in, so to speak, we have a lovely complete set. You could trade in your copy of *Pride and Prejudice* and get that. Provided it's in good condition.'

'Of course,' said the customer, shocked at the idea that anyone could mistreat a book. 'I'll go and look right away.'

Maddy smiled vaguely as the customer bustled off, then jumped as the door opened. 'I'm back,' said Jemma. She was carrying a Rolando's bag and a two-cup holder. 'I got you a soy milk cappuccino.'

'Oh, thank you,' said Maddy, and eased it carefully from the holder. She looked at Jemma. 'Did you have a nice walk?'

'I did, thanks,' said Jemma. 'I know you were meant to go for lunch five minutes ago, but would you mind hanging on for a few minutes more? I need to write down a few things before I forget. Once I'm on the till…'

'Sure,' said Maddy, as the customer returned, holding up *Pride and Prejudice* with the air of someone who had undertaken a challenging quest to find it.

'Thanks,' said Jemma. 'Won't be long.'

'Is that your boss?' said the customer, as the door to the upstairs flat closed behind Jemma. 'She seems young.'

'She's in her mid twenties,' said Maddy. 'I suppose that is young.' Since meeting Luke, she had changed her views on age somewhat. As she was in her mid forties, she had a sneaking suspicion that many people, seeing her and Luke together, assumed she was his mum. Sometimes, truth be told, she did feel she was the responsible half of the relationship. But as Luke was so much older than her, and had experienced many things that she could only imagine and would much rather not, the age gap was too much to think about.

Speaking of things that Maddy would rather not think about, she had a very good idea of where Jemma had been. Given that Luke was determined to chase the Assistant

Keeper job, and that Jemma had waited outside the shop for a few minutes before setting off on her walk, it didn't take a genius to figure it out. But she couldn't tell how the meeting had gone…

She blinked as the customer coughed. 'I'm so sorry. Cash or card, and would you like a bag?'

Jemma came back five minutes later, armed with a notebook, a pack of Post-It notes and a resolute air. Maddy fetched her hummus salad sandwich and raspberry lemonade from the fridge and headed out for a change of scene.

She was itching to text Luke, but he might think she was being nosy. Which she was. So she walked to Soho Square Gardens, found a bench facing a nice tree, and ate her lunch without tasting a mouthful.

She was finishing her lemonade when her phone buzzed. After a splutter, she wiped her mouth and fished the phone from her bag.

I guess that's that.

That's what? she thought. She wanted to shake the phone to get some sense out of it, or rather Luke.

Oh yes? she typed.

Yeah, Jemma as good as said I had no chance.

Her heart leapt. *Oh, I'm sorry. Maybe in the future…*

That's what she said. Doesn't do me any good now though, does it?

It'll all work out, just you wait. Good grief, she sounded like his grandma, not even his mum. *Tell you what, come to mine tonight and I'll make us something nice for dinner. We both deserve a treat.*

Thanks x I'll look forward to it. Love you x

Love you too x

She put the phone in her bag, folded her beeswax sandwich wrap and put her apple core in the bin. *Everything comes to those who wait.*

***

Luke texted again just before five. *I wanted to walk you home but I might be late. Ben took off at 4.45 saying he had an appointment, so I'll have to close up.*

Don't worry about it, Maddy replied. *Come round when you're ready.* Secretly, she was slightly relieved. That would give her time to start dinner, get changed and create a bit of atmosphere. She had already shopped for ingredients in the remainder of her lunch break.

'Doing anything nice tonight?' Jemma asked. She had mostly remained upstairs, but Maddy, who tended to keep the shop laptop open in case of urgent emails or anything interesting on social media, had noticed various things appearing in the calendar. Jemma had added an alert at 5 pm on Friday, labelled *Download applications*. She'd also blocked out two hours on Saturday morning for shortlisting. The following Monday and Tuesday were labelled *Assessment Centre*. She was definitely on the case.

'Luke's coming round for dinner,' said Maddy, putting her phone away.

'Oh, good,' said Jemma. 'Why don't you head off? I can finish here.'

'Are you sure?'

'Yeah.' Jemma grinned. 'Quick, before I change my mind.'

36

Back at the flat, Maddy started the onions and garlic on a low heat. Tonight's meal would be vegan sausage cassoulet, followed by blackcurrant sorbet with sponge fingers and accompanied with a bottle of Chianti. The sorbet and sponge fingers were shop-bought, but still.

She looked around the flat. As soon as she had settled in, Maddy had painted the rooms in various shades of charcoal and dark purple, and invested in long thick curtains, jewel-coloured velvet throws and silver candlesticks from flea markets. A crimson tablecloth and matching chair covers hid the IKEA dining set, and the bedroom was a gloomy haven of rich fabrics.

Just before Luke was due to arrive, she swapped her black top and navy capri pants for a long black dress, teamed with a jet necklace and matching dangly earrings. The doorbell clanged a death knell as she was shaking her hair loose from its plait.

'Hello,' said Luke, and managed a smile. 'You look lovely. I brought these.' He held out a bunch of scarlet roses.

'Oh, lovely. I'll put them in water. Come on in.'

He flopped on the sofa while she found a vase, put the roses on the table and opened the wine. 'Here,' she said, bringing him a silver goblet.

'Thanks.' He took a sip. 'I needed that.'

'Hard day?' she asked, watching him closely.

'You could say that. I knew it was a long shot, and Jemma was nice about it, but... I feel bad. I ought to be ready. I've seen Raphael and Jemma at work, and had opportunities most people never get. And at my age...'

'Oh Luke, you know it doesn't work like that. Anyway, you've got all the time in the world to practise. How many people can say that?'

'I suppose I'm impatient.'

'Yes, you are.' She joined him on the sofa and took a sip from his glass of wine. She snuggled against him and felt him relax. She was relieved it was off the agenda for the time being.

'And after telling me I wasn't ready to be an Assistant Keeper, she tried to send me to Manchester.'

She sat upright and stared at him. 'To do what?'

'For a day trip.'

'Oh.' She snuggled up to him again. 'Why? What's in Manchester?'

'Loads of libraries, apparently. Including one that may or may not have had odd stuff going on.'

Maddy frowned. 'What kind of odd stuff? You aren't going, are you?' She'd experienced enough odd stuff that year to last her a lifetime.

'No.' Luke drank some more wine and put his arm round her. 'It sounded daft. People posting stuff about feeling a bit funny on Facebook. They might have made it up, for all Jemma knows. I said there must be easier ways to find out what's going on than sending me there to hang around. She didn't even want me to do a proper investigation.' Another sip from the glass. 'It's a bit insulting, really.'

'I doubt she meant it like that,' said Maddy. 'Jemma isn't that sort of person.'

'No,' said Luke. 'But my time's worth something, and I

think I do a good job in the shop.'

'You know you do,' said Maddy. 'Everyone would agree. Apart from Ben, obviously.'

'I wonder if he went early for an interview,' said Luke. 'I hope he gets it.'

'Me too,' said Maddy. She kissed him on the cheek, just above where stubble was starting to show. 'I'll check on dinner.'

Everything was progressing as expected, so she cut bread and took it to the table under a cloth, lit the candles and brought the wine. All the while, her heart was singing. Another danger had been averted, and she hadn't even had to intervene. Luke had turned it down by himself.

She topped up the goblet, put the bottle on the table and settled beside Luke. 'Hopefully your documents will arrive any day.'

'They should do,' said Luke. 'Maybe they're waiting for me at the flat.'

'Yes. Then we can finally book things. Oh, and I wanted to talk to you about guests.'

'I thought we had that sorted,' said Luke. 'I mean, it's bookshop people plus your friends and family.'

'It feels . . . unbalanced.' Maddy made a face. 'I know it won't be a formal wedding where you have people on the bride's side or the groom's, but still.'

'My friends will be there,' said Luke. 'It's just that my friends are bookshop people. I mean, obviously all my childhood friends are dead. *Most* of my friends are dead. I was in a bad place before I started at Burns Books. That saved me, really. As for family...'

39

'There's Brian,' said Maddy, after a pause.

'Brian? He was blackmailing me! And yes, he is family, but in the loosest sense. Anyway, he won't come even if he could, which I doubt. Raphael will be there, and Jemma. And you. Surely you don't want to see him again.'

'No, I don't,' said Maddy. 'But he's your great-great nephew. If you do want him to come to the wedding, I'll support that.'

'That's kind of you, but it isn't as if we've kept in touch. The only reason he came to find me was because he wanted something.' Luke rolled the stem of the goblet between his fingers. 'I'll write him a letter, care of Burns Books, and tell him I'm marrying you. That way he knows, and if he wants to send good wishes or a wedding present, he can.'

'That seems fair,' said Maddy. She felt relieved, as if she'd undone an obstinate knot, brushed out a tangle or tidied a messy drawer.

The oven timer pinged and she got up.

Luke stood too. 'I'll set the table.'

'Thanks. Can you bring the trivet?'

Five minutes later, they were sitting at opposite ends of the table with bowls of cassoulet and a goblet each. 'This smells fantastic,' said Luke.

'Thank you.'

Luke got himself some bread and tucked in. Then he looked up. 'Aren't you eating?' He grinned. 'You haven't poisoned it, have you?'

'Don't be silly. I was just thinking… Why isn't Jemma going to Manchester? Normally she's the first to volunteer for a trip.'

'Oh, she's probably busy with recruitment stuff. Although that came after she told me about the Manchester thing. Well, the being in a hurry part did.' Luke studied the table. 'Unless she was offering me a sort of consolation prize.'

'I'm sure that wasn't it,' said Maddy, quickly. 'Even if it was, you saw through it and you're not going.'

'True,' said Luke. But he ate his cassoulet with a pensive air.

CHAPTER 6

Luke strolled towards Charing Cross Library. There was no hurry: Jemma had told him to be there for quarter to ten, and it was just after half nine.

Ben, of course, had kicked up a fuss. 'What do you mean, you won't be in on Monday afternoon or all day Tuesday?'

'Exactly that. I'm helping Jemma with the assessment centre. For the new Assistant Keeper.'

Ben's lip curled to such a degree that Luke wondered if it would ever return to its normal position. 'Load of rubbish if you ask me. What's wrong with an interview?'

'They're being interviewed too, on Monday morning,' said Luke. He thought about adding *So they make sure that this time they recruit someone who's up to the job*, but decided that was tantamount to kicking a man when he was down.

'The quicker they hire someone, the quicker I'm out of here. I'm only staying on as a favour.'

'Oh, right,' said Luke. 'So you've found something?'

'Yeah, or rather, it's found me. A friend from uni wants me to come in on a nice little investment opportunity he's found. Can't tell you what. Hush-hush.' He tapped the side of his nose and gave Luke a wink that made him shudder inwardly. 'Once I leave, I won't be going in a bookshop for a very long time.'

Various rejoinders scurried through Luke's mind, but he contented himself with 'Uh-huh.'

And now he was loping along Charing Cross Road to see how real candidates handled a book emergency.

They'd already lost one of the six. Halfway through the written test on Monday afternoon, which they had held in the stockroom of Burns Books, one of the candidates had had terrible trouble with her pencil.

Each candidate had been issued with one (1) nice sharp pencil, one eraser and one pencil sharpener. They tackled the paper in different ways. One candidate scribbled furiously for the whole time, as if stopping might unleash a terrible curse. Three candidates wrote steadily, with occasional pauses to stare at the ceiling or survey the room. Another candidate, wearing a string of bright pink beads and a turquoise trouser suit, wrote neat short paragraphs illustrated with sketches and marginalia.

The last candidate's pencil broke on every other sentence. The first time, she rolled her eyes, sharpened it and carried on. When it happened again, she scowled at it. The third time, she raised her hand and asked for a replacement, which broke in under a minute. Only then did she (and Luke) realise that the candidates had been given Pencils of Truth to write their answers. She put the broken

43

pencil down and left the stockroom.

Luke, who was helping to invigilate, raised his eyebrows at Jemma, who pursed her lips, collected the paper, glanced at it, then folded it in half in a way that suggested it would not be reopened.

The remaining five candidates would be coming to the library at regular intervals for their practical test. At first, Jemma had been at a loss for a venue. They could have done the test in one of the bookshops, but that would mean closing for the day. 'Where else could we go?' said Jemma.

'What about the local library?' Luke replied. 'It's closed on Tuesdays anyway, so we just need someone to open up.'

'Oooh,' said Jemma. 'But isn't that Rebecca's library? I'm not sure she'd appreciate us staging a book rebellion. Not after what happened a few months ago.'

'A *fake* book rebellion,' said Luke. 'I bet she'll agree if we ask nicely.'

Jemma grinned. 'I bet she would, if *you* asked nicely. If I remember correctly, she was rather taken with you.'

Luke raised his eyebrows. 'I'm not supposed to do that sort of thing any more. Not now I'm engaged.'

'Has Maddy actually said that?'

'Not as such, but—'

'How does a bag of cinnamon rolls from Rolando's sound?'

'A big bag? Go on then.' And they shook on it.

In the end, Luke hadn't had to do much except stand there and smoulder a bit. Jemma had made the request, Rebecca had asked whether Luke would be helping with the assessment and Luke had looked at Jemma, who said 'Oh yes, definitely.'

Rebecca had immediately agreed and volunteered to keep them supplied with tea and coffee. 'Just to make sure that health and safety standards are being met,' she said, toying with the gold chain around her neck. 'Can't be too careful.'

'Absolutely,' said Luke.

Rebecca's free hand made a waving motion that might have been carefree dismissal, or possibly fanning herself.

When Rebecca let him into the library she was wearing a fluffy sweater, pencil skirt and heels. 'I was hoping you'd come early,' she said. 'It's ages since we've spoken.' She sat down and patted the chair next to her. 'We can catch up before the candidates get here.'

'Oh yes,' said Luke. 'What are you doing these days?'

He managed to keep her talking about herself until Jemma appeared five minutes later. Rebecca pouted as Jemma explained that Raphael would be along shortly with some paraphernalia. 'Nothing too full-on, don't worry.'

'I'm glad to hear it,' said Rebecca. 'So what are you planning to do, exactly?'

Jemma took a seat beside Luke and explained. Hopefully she would stick to books and magic, and wouldn't mention that he was getting married...

He was roused from his musings by Raphael's voice. 'So where do I put the killer book?'

Luke looked up and discovered that the Keeper Emeritus had dressed for the occasion in a three-piece suit teamed with a Hawaiian shirt.

'I'm joking,' said Raphael, putting the book he was carrying on the table. 'This book could only cause mild injury, at most.'

'Is *that* a joke?' said Rebecca.

'Maybe a paper cut, or possibly a sore toe if you dropped it on your foot,' said Raphael. 'Anything else our candidates experience is pure imagination.'

***

Luke watched the second candidate approach the book, which was lying on a table in the children's section, smoking gently.

This candidate, a man in his forties dressed in jeans, a white T-shirt and a leather jacket, had brought his own knowledge-emergency kit bag. Jemma had inspected it before the assessment and pronounced it within regulations.

He reached into the bag and brought out a leather gauntlet, which he pulled onto his right hand. Then he assessed the book, crouching to see it better. He held his left hand above the book. 'Warm at most,' he said. 'Doesn't need tongs.' He straightened up and produced a book box from his bag. Then he dropped on one knee and slid the book across the table into the waiting box, which closed with a snap.

He put the box under his arm, took off the gauntlet by gripping the middle finger with his teeth and pulling it free, then reached into the bag for a silver chain and padlock. Ten seconds later, he handed Jemma the chained box and removed the gauntlet from between his teeth. 'There you go.'

'Thank you,' said Jemma, and made a note on her clipboard.

'Is that it? Anything else?'

'That is the end of the assessment,' said Jemma. 'We'll try to get in touch with all the candidates by the end of the day, either way.'

'Great.' He grinned, and Luke blinked. The man's lips were bottle green, and the colour was spreading rapidly over his chin and cheeks. His fingers were green, too. 'I'll be off, then.'

'Before you go,' said Jemma, 'I suggest you wash your hands and face. The toilets are through there.'

The man looked puzzled. 'Why? I mean, the book was a bit dusty, but that's not unusual.'

'Even so, better to be safe than sorry.'

The man glanced at his hand, yelped and ran to the toilet.

'We'll post your equipment to you,' Jemma called. 'Once we've sterilised it.'

'What was *that?*' asked Rebecca.

'An illusion,' said Raphael, with a chuckle. 'The minute water touches him, the colour will vanish. I bet he'll be more careful in future.'

The candidate reappeared, no longer green but moving at a considerably slower pace, and left without another word.

That could easily have been me, thought Luke. *Although I wouldn't have been so confident in the approach. I'd have been more like the first candidate.*

The first candidate was a young woman kitted out in

47

work boots, jeans, knee protectors, a leather jacket and a scarf wound round her neck. Before beginning the test she had tucked her hair inside a woolly hat, then put on surgical gloves and a gas mask. She circled the book for ten minutes, edging slowly closer. When she was within touching distance of it, she pulled on the gauntlet, put a book box on the ground, and produced tongs and a silver chain from her bag. She, at least, could not be faulted on health and safety.

Unfortunately, her hand was shaking too much to grip the book with the tongs. She shunted it this way and that across the table until she moved it slightly over the edge and gripped it that way. The book jerked and she dropped it so that it landed half in and half out of the box. The half in the box crumbled into dust, while the undamaged half whizzed around the library blowing a raspberry, like an escaped balloon.

'I'm so sorry!' she cried, her voice muffled slightly by the gas mask, as they watched the book's erratic progress round the room.

'Don't worry,' said Jemma, putting a consoling hand on her shoulder. 'These things happen.'

The candidate had departed in a flurry, still wearing everything but the mask.

Raphael fidgeted in his chair. 'When is the next candidate coming?'

Jemma checked the time. 'They're due in twenty minutes,' she said. 'If they arrive early, we can always start them off.'

'True,' said Raphael. He picked up the book box the

second candidate had left, undid the padlock and opened the box. He reached in—

'Don't do that!' Luke hurried over, grabbed the box and slammed it shut. 'Give me the chain.'

Raphael raised his eyebrows with an amused expression. 'I appreciate your concern, Luke, but there's no reason to worry. It really is just a book.' He took the box back, opened it and drew out a perfectly normal-looking copy of Mrs Beeton's *Book of Household Management*.

'So I could pick it up and it wouldn't do anything?'

'I wouldn't say that,' said Raphael. 'I've arranged it so that this book will expose candidates' weaknesses. Excessive caution, overconfidence...'

Jemma's mobile buzzed and she frowned. 'I thought I'd diverted this to the shop phone.' She took it from her pocket and checked the screen. 'I must take this,' she said, and hurried out.

'I'll put the kettle on,' said Rebecca. 'I may need help carrying the drinks.' She gave Luke a little smile.

'I'll give you a hand,' said Raphael. 'I don't suppose you have any biscuits?

Luke stayed where he was, sitting on one of the adult-sized chairs they had brought from the main library. His attention drifted outside. If he concentrated, he could hear Jemma. 'No, it's fine, I just wasn't expecting a call,' she said. He strained to catch the voice on the other end of the phone, but that was a step too far.

'What sort of emergency?' said Jemma, and her voice had gone from slightly testy to serious. After a long pause,

49

she said, 'Right. I see why you're concerned, and someone definitely needs to visit you, but that will take a little time to arrange.'

Another brief pause. 'No, I can't come myself. I'm afraid that's out of the question. We're short-staffed as it is. I'm in the middle of a recruitment process to sort that.'

More muffled sounds. 'OK,' said Jemma. 'I promise I'll send someone as soon as I can. No, I can't say when, but I have a little time right now and I'll do my very best. I'll keep you informed. Yes. Goodbye.'

Half a minute later, Jemma hurried into the library and made a beeline for Luke, looking both determined and hopeful. *Here we go again.*

CHAPTER 7

'What's up?' Luke asked, as Rebecca and Raphael came back. Raphael was carrying a tray laden with mugs and a plate of biscuits. 'Tea is served,' he announced grandly. He would have seemed rather like a butler in a grand house if it hadn't been for the Hawaiian shirt.

'Rebecca, would you mind if Luke and I had a quick chat somewhere?' asked Jemma. 'I've had a worrying phone call and I need to fill Luke in.'

Rebecca's eyebrows rose. 'There's the meeting room. It's not as grand as it sounds, mind you.'

'It'll just be a quick chat.'

We'll see, thought Luke, as he stood. *I may not be the pushover you think.*

'Take your drinks,' said Raphael. 'I assume you don't need me.'

'Thanks for the offer, but I can manage,' said Jemma. 'If the next candidate comes before we're done, please fetch us. I'd prefer to get this sorted as soon as possible.'

'It isn't...' Rebecca looked worried. 'It isn't a local

matter, is it? Like the – the other trouble?'

'No, it's in another region,' said Jemma.

'Oh. OK.' Rebecca's worry transformed into relief. 'I'll take you to the room.'

The meeting room would have been a tight fit for four people. Even a coffee table and two chairs seemed too big for it. Luke wondered what on earth the library staff used it for.

'Take a seat,' said Jemma. 'I'll get to the point. I've had a phone call from one of the staff at John Rylands Library.'

'Oh yes?' Luke adopted an expression of polite interest. 'Have more people been sticking to the floor?'

Jemma frowned at him. 'It's not funny, Luke. Whatever you think of Facebook groups or the people who post in them, some of it is genuine. It's not all people making stuff up for kicks, or clicks. Jess, the woman I've been speaking to, is really worried. She's one of the library assistants there.'

'So did *she* stick to the floor?'

'Luke, be serious.' Jemma sighed. 'Basically, she was shelving books yesterday in one of the reading-room galleries when she heard banging below.'

'OK… Was someone trying to get in, or out?'

'I'll come to that. She said it was a sort of thumping and rattling. And the library is closed to visitors on Mondays, so it couldn't have been someone hiding or messing around. Anyway, Jess looked over the balcony to work out what it was. At first she couldn't see anything, then realised something was happening with the bookshelves. They're glass-fronted, to preserve the books.

Which were thumping at the glass.'

Luke's eyebrows shot up.

'Jess ran downstairs and shouted at the books to stop it, but they wouldn't. She was worried that they would break the glass, but she didn't know what to do. She locked the door of the reading room and went to fetch her boss, but when they came back, the books were sitting on the shelves as normal.'

'Riiiight.' Luke's brow furrowed. 'And you believe her?'

'Here's the thing,' said Jemma. 'Before she left the room, Jess took a quick video. She sent me a private link.' She pulled out her phone.

Luke watched as leather-bound volumes thudded against glass, over and over. Some books moved in a cluster, others independently, chafing their neighbours. 'Woah,' he breathed.

'Quite,' said Jemma. 'She showed her boss, Yvonne, and they agreed the best thing to do was keep the reading room locked today and as long as needed. Obviously, that isn't ideal.'

'So what took them so long to get in touch?' asked Luke. 'Why did they ring you? What about this Ludovic character?'

'I didn't hear the whole story,' said Jemma. 'My impression was that they couldn't get hold of Ludovic.' A brief smile. 'I'm glad it's not just me. Apparently they went into the director's office and found a Rolodex, of all things, with my number in it. So...' She gave Luke a beseeching look. 'Please will you head up and see what's going on?'

Luke was silent for a moment, choosing his words. 'I don't mean to be awkward, Jemma,' he said, 'but why me? Why can't you or Raphael go? Either of you would be much more likely to fix whatever it is.'

'Before we get to that,' said Jemma, 'can I ask what's stopping you from agreeing to this?'

Damn, thought Luke. 'Honestly?'

'Honestly. I'm aware you thought it was small potatoes when I asked you at first, but things are clearly escalating. So this really would be a development opportunity for you.'

Luke drank some tea, which was already going cold. 'First, I don't know Manchester. Not at all. I'm suspicious of unfamiliar places. Secondly, I'm not sure about the train journey. I've never gone on a long train journey. It might be fine, or something might trigger a – an episode. I don't want *that* to happen when I'm stuck on a train for three hours.'

'OK.' Jemma picked up her own mug, sipped and made a face. 'The second one is easy, and maybe the first one is too. You can borrow Gertrude. You've travelled in her and you'll have plenty of space.'

'There's one problem,' said Luke. 'I can't drive. No licence, remember.'

Jemma grinned. 'Maddy can.'

'*Maddy?*'

'Yes, why not?'

'She's… She *can* drive, but I don't know how she'd feel about taking a camper van up north. She's no fan of motorways.'

'Gertrude would take the strain,' said Jemma. 'It's more a matter of Maddy sitting in the driver's seat and holding the steering wheel. And if she went with you, that would help with the Manchester thing. You wouldn't be on your own in a strange city.'

'What makes you think she'll want to go to Manchester and prowl round a library?'

'Ahh,' said Jemma. 'Let me show you something.' Her thumbs flew over her phone and she brought up a gallery of images. 'This is the library.' She handed him the phone.

Luke glanced at the first image and whistled. 'You're kidding me.'

'No, that's it. Smack in the middle of the city.'

The photo showed a building which looked more like a cathedral than a library. Pointed windows, delicate carving, dark, warm stone that could have been there for a thousand years... Luke's mouth watered.

'Scroll down,' said Jemma. 'There's the reading room.'

Luke stared at the image. Arches rose into the air, with balconies, and below were alcoves filled with bookshelves. Light filtered in through lots of windows, some with stained glass. He kept scrolling and found carvings, grand staircases, statues...

He looked at Jemma. 'You could have told me this before.'

'I didn't think of it before,' said Jemma. 'It was a nice-to-do thing then. Now, I really need you to go. Think of it as a sort of mini-break. I'll pay your expenses, of course, within reason: I don't expect you to sleep in Gertrude. I could even give you a bonus, maybe.'

Luke wondered whether, if he sat tight, he could secure a promotion. 'What about the bookshops while we're away?'

'Ben and I can manage all that,' said Jemma. 'If Ben won't play ball, Em can help. Carl too, at a pinch. It would do him good to get his head out of his manuscript. That Arts Council bursary was a double-edged sword—'

A tap at the door. 'Sorry to disturb you,' said Rebecca's voice, 'but Hermione Dawes has arrived.'

'Oh good,' said Jemma. 'We'll be right there.' She gave Luke a look which said, as clearly as words, *To be continued.*

Hermione Dawes turned out to be the woman with the pink beads, which were now teamed with a cream blouse, black trousers and loafers. Jemma explained the task and Raphael handed her a knowledge-emergency kit bag, which she checked. 'OK, I'm ready,' she said.

'In that case,' said Raphael, 'I shall produce the book.' He opened a book box and set the smoking book on the small table.

Hermione stood, walked over to the table, crouched beside it and inspected the book. 'OK, it doesn't smell funny and it isn't burning.' She brought her hand close to it to make sure. 'Excuse me,' she said to the book. 'Are you all right?' Her voice was calm, enquiring.

A fat puff of smoke issued from the book.

'I guess that's a no. Are you cross?'

Luke could feel the increasing warmth from his seat.

'I'd love to help,' said Hermione, 'but I'm not sure

what you want. Shall we say one puff for yes and two puffs for no?'

A small puff of smoke.

'Are you tired?'

A wisp of grey rose from the cover.

'Would you like to rest?'

The book emitted a more emphatic plume.

'OK.' Hermione took the book box from her kit bag, thought for a moment, then reached for her handbag, which had a polka-dot scarf knotted around the strap. She untied it and kept it in her hand. 'You can rest in this box,' she said. 'Shall I leave the lid open?'

One more puff.

'Right. On the count of three, I'm going to wrap you in the scarf, pick you up and put you in the box. One . . . two . . . three.' She wrapped the book in a smooth, unhurried movement, lifted it and settled it in the box. For a few moments, she watched it. No smoke rose, and the temperature was normal. She stood. 'There you go.'

'Nice work, Hermione,' said Jemma.

'Thanks,' said Hermione. 'I did a counselling skills evening class a few months ago and wondered if I could apply it to low-level book emergencies. Turns out you can, if you're careful.'

'That was really interesting,' said Raphael. 'Perhaps our more disruptive books would benefit from listening sessions.'

Luke gazed at Hermione. Outwardly, she seemed a perfectly normal young woman, but he had a distinct feeling that he was looking at his new senior colleague.

And he was fine with that. *I could learn a lot from her*, he thought.

'That's the end of the assessment, Hermione,' said Jemma. 'We'll aim to contact you with a decision by the end of the day. We have two more candidates to see this afternoon, so expect a call by five.'

'I'll head off, then,' said Hermione. 'Admin calls.' She rolled her eyes and shook hands with them all in turn.

Jemma unwrapped the book gently and gave Hermione her scarf. 'Would you be prepared to do a presentation at one of our learning meetings?'

'If it doesn't involve slides, yes.' She smiled. 'I'll let you get on.'

When Hermione had gone, Raphael said, 'She's the one to beat.'

'That was pretty cool,' said Rebecca. 'I'd be interested in learning that too. Not so much for books as for my teenager.'

Jemma was silent for a moment. 'OK, our next candidate isn't due until two, so I suggest we break for lunch and come back then. Luke, I'll walk to Burns Books with you.'

They were well on the way when she spoke again. 'I imagine you can guess what I'm going to ask you.'

Luke felt as if things had shifted in his head, first when Jemma had shown him the library and then when he had watched Hermione handle the book. 'Before I answer, I'd still like to know why you or Raphael can't go.'

Jemma gave him a long look. 'OK. This goes no further than you and me. Understand?'

He nodded.

'Raphael *could* go, but I'm worried about the effect it might have on him. The magical elements of his role take a toll: that's why he stepped away from the Keeper position. If something happened to Raphael, I'd never forgive myself.' Her mouth curled at the corner. 'Also, Giulia would kill me.'

'Why not you, then?'

'That's probably easier to understand. It's not medical advice as such, but I've been told not to get involved in any book emergencies beyond basic ones for the near future. Hence my rush to appoint an Assistant Keeper.'

Luke stared at her. 'You mean you're not well? Why didn't you say?'

'Oh, for heaven's sake, Luke. I'm not ill. I'm fine. But... I'm pregnant.'

CHAPTER 8

Maddy was restocking the shelves when Jemma returned to the Friendly Bookshop. 'How did the assessments go?' Maddy asked, from her perch on the little stepladder.

'Pretty well,' said Jemma. 'One very strong candidate I'd be happy to appoint, which takes the heat off. Have you been busy?'

Maddy shelved the last two books and climbed down. 'I've hardly stopped. I've taken two full boxes of books out of the stockroom so far, and we've still got gaps.'

'Wow. That's amazing, for a Tuesday. Why don't you go for lunch? Take a long one: I don't need to be at the library until two, and it isn't far. Oh, and Luke wants to see you.'

Maddy smiled. 'I should hope so.' She fetched her lunch from the fridge and got her coat and bag. 'Can I get you anything before I go? Cup of tea?'

'No, I haven't long had one. Go on, off you go.'

Maddy walked to Burns Books feeling pleased with life. On one hand, she liked having the shop to herself, so that she could arrange the books the way she wanted them and they'd stay that way for a little while. However, she also liked selling books and chatting with customers, and knowing the shop was doing well made her happy.

She entered Burns Books to find Luke serving a customer at the ground-floor counter. 'Where's Ben?' she asked, once the customer had left.

'Out to lunch,' said Luke, with a grin. 'When I came in I found Em working here. She'll take over when I go to lunch, then take her break when Ben gets back. If he ever does. Honestly.'

'You're remarkably chirpy, considering.'

'Wouldn't you be?'

'Um, not particularly. I'm just glad I don't have to work with Ben on a daily basis.'

'Not that!' Luke gave her a quizzical look. 'You've spoken to Jemma, right?'

'Yes, she said I could take my lunch. And that you wanted to see me.'

'Oh.' Luke seemed both surprised and slightly disappointed. Then he brightened. 'In that case, I'll text Em. Let's go out.'

'Didn't you bring lunch?'

'Yes, but I fancy going out. I'll get a hot dog.'

Maddy made a face. 'That's probably even worse than what you normally have.' She sighed. 'Come on.'

As threatened, Luke bought a hot dog from a stall in the park, smothered it in ketchup and mustard, and made short work of it. 'How can something be wonderful and disgusting at the same time?' he asked, as he wiped his mouth and threw the napkin in a nearby bin.

'Don't ask me,' said Maddy. 'Let's sit down. I don't fancy my chances eating a salad on the move.'

They sat on the next bench and Maddy brought out the layered salad she had prepared the night before, plus a carton of apple juice. 'Go on then,' she said, as she unwrapped a bamboo fork. 'Tell me why you're so bouncy.'

'You know that trip Jemma wanted me to go on? To Manchester?'

'Yeees…'

'It's got more serious, so I'm going. And she wants you to come too.'

'Me?' Maddy gawped at him. 'Why do I need to go?'

'To look after me. Well, not exactly. I was worried about going on the train and being alone in a strange city. So Jemma said you could come and we could take Gertrude.'

'So I'm babysitting you? What about the bookshops?'

'Jemma can sort those out. It'll be fine. Anyway…' Luke found a picture on his phone. 'This is the library. You'll love it.'

'Wow,' said Maddy, gazing at a photo of the reading room. 'So that's real? Not AI, or Photoshop?'

'No, it's real, and I saw more photos. The outside's unbelievable. Hang on.'

'That is a very cool building,' said Maddy. 'If it was in London, I'd definitely go. I don't fancy going north and playing detective.'

'It won't be like that,' said Luke. He gazed at her, looking rather hurt, then bit his lip. 'I'm not sure I can do it without you.'

Immediately, Maddy felt a pang of guilt. Luke kept gazing at her, his eyes pale-green pools of disappointment. 'Wait a minute,' she said. 'Are you doing a glamour thing on me?'

Luke looked even more hurt. 'No!' He put a hand on her arm. 'I don't want to manipulate you into going if you really don't want to. But I thought – I thought you might like to come on a trip with me. You don't have to do anything. I mean, you don't have to do magic or investigate. You'd be in a sort of . . . support role.'

'Thanks a lot.' She speared some salad and chewed vigorously.

Luke spread his hands. 'What should I say? First you don't want to do any actual work, then when I say you don't have to, that's wrong too.'

Maddy swallowed her food and prepared another fork of virtuousness. 'It's a pretty abrupt about-turn, you must admit. What's brought this on?'

'The situation's more serious, for one thing,' said Luke. 'It's not just me pretending to be a tourist and checking out the vibes. Jemma's lending us Gertrude, and she'll give us a bonus, and basically it's a paid mini-break with a bit of work. What's not to like?' He held Maddy's gaze and smiled. 'Also, I need you to drive Gertrude.'

'Right, now you're definitely doing the glamour thing.'

'Sorry,' said Luke. 'Didn't mean to.'

'Apology accepted,' said Maddy. 'Let me think about it. It sounds nice, but I bet there are strings attached.'

'OK,' said Luke. 'That's fair. It would be lovely if you

63

did come along.'

Maddy studied him. 'So you're definitely going, with or without me.'

He looked shamefaced. 'Yes. I said I'd do it. I can take the train: apparently the journey isn't that long. I can always sit in the toilet if I'm . . . worried.'

'All right,' said Maddy, and carried on eating her lunch.

'We could treat it as a sort of test,' said Luke, a few minutes later.

Maddy's fork froze halfway to her mouth. 'Excuse me?'

'If I hate it, at least I'll know I'm not cut out to be an Assistant Keeper, and I won't have had to go through the whole interview process. If you come too, it's sort of the same thing.'

Maddy gave him a withering look. 'I don't want to be an Assistant Keeper, Luke. I want to sell books, keep the shop tidy, and get on with my colleagues.'

'OK,' said Luke. 'I'll shut up. Oh, except... Could I borrow a suitcase from you?'

Maddy's blood turned to ice in her veins. 'When are you going?'

'Tomorrow morning. I told you things are getting more serious.'

'Of course you can,' she said, and the words didn't feel like hers. 'Will you go home and pack?'

Luke nodded.

She snapped the lid onto her salad box. 'I should go back to the shop.'

'Maddy, it'll be fine. I can take care of myself.'

'I know you can. I've got – things to think about. I'll

see you later, anyway. We can go to mine together.' She kissed him on the cheek and stood up.

The shop was mercifully quiet that afternoon. Jemma returned at a quarter to four and asked for half an hour's grace to do recruitment admin.

'Sure,' said Maddy. 'Can I ask... Luke told me about the Manchester thing at lunchtime.'

'Oh yes,' said Jemma. 'I thought he would.'

'I'm surprised you didn't mention it to me when you came back from the library.'

'I considered it,' said Jemma. 'I figured it would come better from Luke. See you later.' And she was off upstairs before Maddy could reply.

Luke was quiet when he came to collect her, too. 'Jemma appointed someone, then,' she said, for something to say.

'Yes.' He seemed a thousand miles away.

'The right person?'

'Oh yeah. She was . . . inspiring.'

Maddy wasn't sure she liked the sound of that. 'In what way?'

'She was so good with the book. She'd really thought about it, you could tell.'

'Oh, right.'

When they reached the flat, Maddy pulled her suitcase from the cupboard her landlord had built in a dark corner. It was a black hard-shell case with a twist of purple ribbon round the handle. 'You can untie that if you want,' she said, pointing to the ribbon.

'No, I like it,' said Luke. 'It reminds me of you.'

Maddy laughed. 'I won't ask. Do you fancy a tea? Coffee? I could open a bottle of wine…'

'No, I'd better go and pack.' He was already heading for the door.

'When do you leave in the morning? I'll come and see you off.'

'It's OK, you'll probably be at the shop by then. Here…' He put his arms around her and held her tight, then kissed the top of her head. 'I'll be back before you know I'm gone.'

'Even so, a proper kiss, if you don't mind.'

When he had gone, Maddy pottered, straightening ornaments, dusting the mantelpiece, rearranging the shoes on the rack. She put on music to feel less alone.

You could go with him.

She pushed the thought away. *I don't like new things.*

Luke was a new thing once.

She turned the music up.

Half an hour later, she heard buzzing. It was her phone, sitting on the coffee table.

He wants to borrow something else. He'll try to persuade me again. She hardened her heart as she walked to the table.

The message was one word: *Look!*

She clicked on the attachment. It was a photo of Luke's new passport and birth certificate. His new birth date was August 8, 2000. They'd chosen it together: 8 August was the date when Dracula had arrived in England.

The phone buzzed. *They finally came! I'm a legal person!*

66

Great! she replied. *Now we can get things moving.*

She frowned. *He does want to get things moving, doesn't he?*

Three dots bounced, then another message appeared. *Yes, when I'm back from Manchester.*

***

The process of making Luke legal had been torturous, largely because it was so uncommon. Luke had done some research and got nowhere. Then Raphael had put him in touch with Sergeant Hawkins of the City of London Police, whom they had met briefly during the crisis a few months before. Luke had had to supply all sorts of information – full name, date and place of birth, date of becoming undead, any criminal convictions, date of any previous marriages, previous addresses for the last hundred years – and ask Jemma and Raphael for character references.

Two weeks later, he had met her for lunch and shown her a strange email. 'It's really happening,' he said, though he looked nervous rather than happy, and handed her his phone. The subject line of the email was *SURRENDER*.

STRICTLY CONFIDENTIAL
Dear Mr Varney,

You are required to surrender any existing birth or marriage certificates and any passports in your possession. They will be kept securely in the files of the committee.

Please place all documents in a brown envelope and put them in the night safe outside Cadwallader's Bank,

67

Giltspur Street, Farringdon Without between 8.45 and 9 pm tonight.

If you have no documents of this type, please submit a postcard or a stuck-down envelope with your full name, your signature, and the word UNDOCUMENTED.

Yours sincerely,
Legalisation Committee

Maddy had come with him that night, full of excitement and some guilt. 'Are you sure you don't mind?' she asked more than once, as they threaded their way through the quiet streets.

'Why would I mind?' He had chosen a postcard of Trafalgar Square to make his declaration. It seemed strangely appropriate.

'It's as if you're getting rid of your former self.'

'I don't think of it like that. I'm becoming a new person. A *legal* person. I can get married and go abroad if I want. Or claim benefits, or see a doctor. Or even learn to drive.'

Cadwallader's Bank was a once-imposing building whose stone mouldings were blunted by age. Luke stepped up to the night safe and took the postcard from his inner jacket pocket.

Maddy took it for a moment, kissed it, kissed him, then gave back the postcard. 'Thank you,' she said. 'This is probably the nicest thing anyone's ever done for me.'

'Oh, you…' He put an arm round her, then inspected the night safe. 'Surely this needs a key…'

He tugged the handle and the night safe yawned open

with a grudging creak, revealing a wedge-shaped cavity. He dropped in the postcard. 'Well, that's it, I guess,' he said, and closed it with a clang that seemed final. He tried to reopen it, to see whether the postcard had gone anywhere, but it was stuck fast. 'One shot, then.'

'Yes,' Maddy had replied. 'I'm so proud of you.'

***

He went through all that for me, she thought, looking at the photo of Luke's brand-new passport and birth certificate.

I want him to be proud of me, too.

She put her phone on the table and paced for a minute or two. Questions were jostling in her head.

What if I don't like it?

What if something scary happens?

What if Luke's hurt, and I could have stopped it by being there?

What if he doesn't come back?

She grabbed the phone. *I hope I don't regret this*, she thought.

Leave room in that suitcase, she typed. *And text Jemma to cancel your train ticket. I'm coming with you.*

CHAPTER 9

Maddy's alarm shrilled in what felt like the dead of night. Luke squeezed his eyelids shut, hoping it was a bad dream, but the noise continued.

Maddy rolled over and silenced it, then got up and put on her dressing gown.

'What time is it?'

'Six o'clock,' said Maddy.

He blinked. 'Why so early?'

'Better early than late. And you'll need a good breakfast before we leave.'

Then he remembered. Their expedition to Manchester, which Maddy was now part of. *It's happening.*

He propped himself on one elbow and watched her move about the room. Then he threw off the covers and found last night's T-shirt.

'We'll eat first,' said Maddy. 'The noise of the shower might wake Mrs Grabowski upstairs. It doesn't take much.' She opened the bedroom door. 'Coffee?'

'Yes, please. Decaf.'

Twenty minutes later, he was sitting in front of a steak and mushroom sandwich. Maddy had cut it in half, and pinkish meat juices were seeping onto the plate. It was making his mouth water. 'Are you sure you don't mind?' he asked.

She shrugged. 'It'll set you up for the day. Anyway, I've cooked it, which was the worst bit.' She managed to smile. 'The least you can do is eat it, then it's done with.'

'Fair enough.' He picked up half the sandwich and took a bite. 'This is great,' he said, through the sandwich.

'Good.' Maddy sipped her black coffee. She had two slices of wholemeal toast with peanut butter, an apple and a banana. 'When I finish this, I'll pack lunch for the journey. Plus snacks. We have to have snacks on a road trip, and I've got a fresh box of teabags.'

'They do have food in Manchester,' Luke said, as soon as he was able. 'And there are service stations on the way.'

'Have you ever eaten at a service station?' asked Maddy. 'If you have, you'll know why I've packed food.' She finished her breakfast, went into the kitchen, got supplies from the fridge and started making sandwiches.

Luke watched her as he breakfasted. While he was pleased at Maddy's change of heart, he also felt puzzled.

When he'd received her text last night, he had replied. *Great! When I've packed, I'll bring the suitcase to yours.* He considered adding *What made you change your mind?* Then he decided that probably wasn't a question to ask via his phone.

When he arrived at Maddy's, she gave him a hug and took him into the bedroom, where a little pile of clothes sat on the bed, along with two books, a pair of flat shoes and a small first-aid kit. 'I'll pack toiletries in the morning,' she said. 'My phone is charging and I have a spare cable. Did you bring yours?'

'I knew there was something,' he said, feeling superfluous to requirements. 'Um, can I ask you a question?'

'Would you put the suitcase on the bed for me?'

'Sure.' He undid the clasps and opened the case.

Maddy looked inside, refolded a pair of trousers, then began adding her belongings. 'There,' she said. 'What did you want to ask me?'

'What made you change your mind?'

'Oh.' She considered for a few moments. 'It seemed the right thing to do.'

Luke studied Maddy's back as she made sandwiches and wrapped them, prepared a salad and put it in a tub, then made a flask of decaf tea. Her quiet efficiency surprised him. Not that Maddy was ever inefficient, but he hadn't expected her to get on with the preparations without any need to refer to him. *Is she doing all this to stop herself thinking about what's ahead? I hope she won't get cold feet. What would we do then?* He imagined Maddy frozen outside the library, or trembling in a corner.

As arranged in a flurry of texts between him and Jemma the previous evening, they arrived at the Friendly Bookshop just before half past seven. The light was already on. Luke wondered if he should knock, given the early hour, but Maddy said 'It's too cold to stand here,' opened the door and went in.

Jemma and Raphael were talking at the counter, on which was a sealed cardboard box, two knowledge-emergency kit bags and a Burns Books tote. Folio was also on the counter, rubbing his chin against a corner of the box.

They looked up as the pair came in. 'Bright and early, I see,' said Raphael.

'Early, definitely,' said Luke. 'Maddy's a lot brighter than me.'

'It's a good thing she's driving, then,' said Raphael. 'Although Gertrude will take the strain.'

Maddy shrank a little and Luke put an arm around her shoulders. He could feel the tension running through her. 'It'll be fine, Maddy. Gertrude's a very smart van.'

'I'm sure she is,' said Maddy. 'Are there paper bags in the glove box?'

'There will be,' said Jemma. 'We have supplies for you.' She patted the cardboard box. 'We put some books in here, for a plausible alternative reason to be at the library. Don't open it unless you have to. The bookshop will decide what books you need.'

'Will it be able to do that when we're . . . a long way away?'

Raphael shrugged. 'Anything's possible.'

'You know what these are,' said Jemma, touching the kit bags. 'I've given you one each. Hopefully you won't require a spare.'

Maddy looked at Luke, her eyes practically all pupil. She turned to Jemma. 'What's in the tote?'

'Two Pencils of Truth, well sharpened, two notebooks,

an A to Z of Greater Manchester, and a bag of Rolando's cinnamon rolls for the journey.'

'The best travel-sickness preventative there is,' Raphael added, and Folio purred.

'I suppose we'd better get moving,' said Luke.

'Not so fast,' said Jemma. 'I said I'd give you both a bonus for doing this, and Raphael and I thought it should take the form of an acting position. Therefore, until your return, you are both Acting Associate Keepers. Congratulations.' She shook hands with first Maddy, then Luke. He started as warmth flowed from Jemma's hand to his, spreading up his arm and through his body. Then he glanced at Maddy, who seemed rather affronted.

'Hang on a minute,' he said. 'What's an Associate Keeper?' *Have I bitten off more than I can chew?*

'We're hoping you'll tell us that,' said Raphael. For a moment, Luke wondered if Raphael had read his thoughts. 'It certainly means that you are temporarily members of the Keepers' Guild, with the associated privileges and protections.'

Luke stared at him. 'So we're both immortal?'

'Technically, no. Practically, yes, unless you get into a far worse situation than we anticipate.'

Luke saw Maddy's eyes widen. 'Which won't happen,' he said firmly.

'Absolutely,' said Jemma, with an encouraging smile at them both. 'I've booked you an Airbnb for tonight and I'll text you the address. If you need to stay another night, just let me know.'

'I'll bring Gertrude round,' said Raphael, jingling a set

of keys. He strode towards the shop door, and Luke noticed he was wearing blue and white striped pyjama trousers with his tweed jacket, pink shirt and blue silk cravat.

Jemma and Maddy chatted about the weather forecast and the journey time. Luke gazed through the shop window, his heart too full for speech. *This is my big chance*, he thought. *I can't blow it.*

Two minutes later, a familiar orange shape pulled into view and Folio meowed.

'I guess it's time,' said Maddy. She picked up a kit bag, slung the tote over her shoulder and took the handle of the suitcase. Luke took the other kit bag and hefted the box of books, which was surprisingly light.

Outside, dawn was breaking. Raphael jumped out of the vehicle and opened the back doors. 'Probably best to stow things under the seats. You'll want the tote with you, though.'

They put their things in, then Raphael opened the driver's door for Maddy. She hesitated for a moment before climbing up to the seat. 'I thought I'd have to adjust this.'

'Gertrude's very accommodating,' said Raphael. 'I've already put the address into the satnav.' He pointed to the round grey screen which normally sat behind the clock dial. On it, in green capitals, were the words *John Rylands Library, Deansgate, Manchester.*

'So we're really going,' said Maddy, in a small voice.

Luke opened the passenger door and got in. 'Yes: we're going on an adventure.'

'Take care of them, won't you,' said Raphael.

Luke wondered who he was talking to, then realised it

must be Gertrude. 'We'll take care of her, too,' he said.

'Take care of yourselves,' said Jemma. 'Don't do anything silly. And if you need help or advice, phone or text. Promise?'

'Promise,' they chorused.

'In that case, have a good trip!' Jemma and Raphael stepped back, waving.

Maddy put the van in gear, took the handbrake off and indicated.

'Wave for me,' she muttered. 'I can't look round.' Her knuckles were white as she gripped the steering wheel.

Gertrude glided forward. Maddy checked the mirrors several times, then eased the van into the road.

Luke turned in his seat and waved as Jemma and Raphael grew smaller and smaller, and finally disappeared. He settled in his seat and blew out a puff of air. 'We're on the way.'

'Yes,' said Maddy, not taking her eyes off the road.

The satnav led them left along Euston Road, then to the A40. 'Have you noticed?' said Maddy.

'Noticed what?' Luke looked up from the *Greater Manchester A to Z.*

'All the traffic lights are green.'

'Oh yes, that's one of Gertrude's things. Although it is quieter than usual at this time of day.'

They reached the M40 surprisingly quickly and Maddy guided the camper van onto the motorway. 'So far so good,' she said. After a few minutes, she overtook a slow-moving lorry. 'If motorways were always like this, I wouldn't mind them.'

'They're only like this when you're in Gertrude,' said Luke. 'Unfortunately.'

Maddy pulled out to overtake a Mini. 'I might as well stay in the middle lane,' she said. 'There's so much slow traffic in the inside lane. I'm doing sixty-five, and I'm whizzing past all these cars.'

Luke kept quiet.

'I can't be at the turn-off already,' said Maddy. 'I didn't think we'd be out of London yet, never mind heading for the Midlands.'

In due course they travelled down the M42, then reached the M6 Toll, where they discovered that Gertrude, as a very special classic camper van, was exempt from the toll fee.

Maddy checked the satnav dial as Gertrude merged into a motorway lane. 'This says it's the M6 proper next.'

'That sounds about right,' said Luke. 'How are you finding Gertrude to drive?'

'Easy,' said Maddy. 'Suspiciously so.' She was quiet for a few moments as they overtook a white Transit van. 'What time is it?' she asked.

Luke checked his phone. 'Just after half eight.'

'Don't be daft, it can't be.'

'Magical van,' Luke replied. 'I bet she's got as much petrol in the tank as she had when we started.'

Maddy checked the fuel gauge and huffed. 'I suppose I should be glad that I don't have to pay service-station prices,' she said. 'But honestly.'

They cruised until they reached Princess Parkway. Ahead were the tall buildings of Manchester, silhouetted against a cloudy sky.

They opened the windows for some air and caught an odd, sweetish smell. 'That must be the brewery,' said Luke, pointing.

Gertrude moved smoothly from lane to lane, negotiating corners and passing through green lights all the way to Deansgate.

'I'm not sure about parking,' said Luke. 'I checked the library website and they said it doesn't have a car park.'

'Gertrude will know exactly where to go,' said Maddy. After a moment, she patted the steering wheel.

The library peeped out from behind tall buildings, then grew bigger. On the satnav, a green arrow pointed right. Maddy entered a narrow street with double yellow lines on both sides. 'I hope you know what you're doing,' she told the satnav.

The van crept down the side of the library. Luke checked on either side for a likely place, but the spaces he could see were marked *Private Parking*.

Gertrude rolled gently to a stop and another green arrow appeared. This time, it was pointing to approximately seven o'clock on the dial.

'Does she want me to turn round?' asked Maddy. 'There isn't room. Not for a van.'

Luke looked over his shoulder. 'Oh! There's a space at the back of the library, and a sign which says *Authorised Vehicles Only*.'

'Is Gertrude an authorised vehicle?' asked Maddy.

'She thinks she is.'

'Fine.' Maddy put the van in reverse. 'If we get in

trouble, I'll say it was your idea,' she told the steering wheel.

The van glided backwards and the wheel moved between Maddy's hands. 'This is weird,' she said, as Gertrude moved into the space. 'And we haven't even tackled what's in the library yet.'

'We'll cross that bridge when we come to it,' said Luke.

Maddy put the handbrake on, turned off the engine and took the keys from the ignition. 'Do we need to take anything with us?'

'I'd like to say no,' said Luke. 'But we should take in the kit bags and the tote. And I wouldn't mind a cinnamon roll before we go in.'

'Neither would I,' said Maddy. 'Even though it's...' She closed the clock over the satnav screen. 'Nine twenty, apparently.' She looked faintly exasperated.

They shared a cup of tea from the flask and ate two cinnamon rolls each. *I can't put it off for ever*, thought Luke. *I have to face whatever is in there. It may not be as bad as I think.* Now he was actually outside the library and the test was imminent, the cinnamon rolls sat like lead in his stomach.

'Right.' Maddy opened the door and jumped down. 'Let's find out what's going on.' And Luke had no choice but to follow.

CHAPTER 10

As they walked along the narrow road towards the library entrance, Luke checked his shirt was tucked in and settled his collar. He wished he'd worn a suit jacket, but it was too late. Maddy was dressed in her usual bookshop uniform: cotton trousers and a striped boat-necked top, with her hair in a plait.

Maddy held out her hand. 'It'll be fine,' she said, and smiled at him. He returned the smile, hoping she was right.

They reached the main road, turned right, and walked past what must be the original entrance of the library: a pair of huge doors in an arched frame. The new entrance was a sliding door leading into a sort of vestibule, in a glass extension on the side. More importantly, it was closed.

'Of course.' Luke raked a hand through his hair and huffed. 'The library doesn't open until ten.'

Maddy peered in. 'Well, people are inside.' She rapped on the glass.

Heads whipped round and Luke almost stepped back.

They must be jumpy.

A petite black-haired woman in a purple fleece and black trousers walked to the glass, mouthing *We're closed.*

Luke and Maddy exchanged glances.

The woman disappeared, then reappeared in the vestibule and the glass door slid open. 'I'm afraid we don't open until ten o'clock,' she said. 'There are lots of coffee shops round here, though.'

'I'm sorry, we're a bit early,' said Luke. 'We've come about the reading room. Jemma James sent us.'

'Oh! I'm so sorry. Do come in.' Immediately she opened the door wide, ushered them in and locked it. 'We knew you were coming, but we weren't sure when. It's Luke, isn't it?' She regarded Maddy with a puzzled expression.

'This is Maddy, my . . . colleague. We're both Associate Keepers from London.' Luke tried to remember what Jemma had told him of the case, but his brain wasn't cooperating. Then a name flashed into his mind. 'Would you be Jess?'

'I'm Soraya. Jess is busy upstairs in Reader Services.' She led them into the foyer, and two other staff looked at them while pretending not to.

'Perhaps we could start by interviewing Jess, to get a picture of what we're dealing with.'

'I take your point,' said Soraya, 'but Ludovic was very clear that he wanted to speak to you before any investigation began. Ludovic's the Assistant Keeper for Manchester.'

'Oh yes, Jemma mentioned—'

'He's actually in the director's office. If you wouldn't mind waiting, I'll phone and tell him you've arrived.' She scurried behind the desk without waiting to see if they would comply.

The foyer of the library was part reception, part gift shop. It was also disappointingly modern, all white walls and floor-to-ceiling windows. Luke wandered from table to table, looking at pen nibs, notebooks, enamel pins. There were a couple of pins Maddy would like – in fact, he was surprised she wasn't by his side. She was at the reception desk, chatting to another member of staff. He found himself frowning. Not that he minded Maddy chatting to people. It just wasn't *her*. She tended to keep herself to herself and be reserved, even with people she knew.

Soraya put the phone down. 'His phone's ringing out. I'll ring round a few other departments, see if he's there.'

Luke walked to the reception desk. 'So is the reading room still closed?' asked Maddy.

'Oh yes,' said the long-faced young man she was talking to. *Maddy, approaching a young man?* he thought. *Very unusual.* 'You couldn't possibly risk a member of the public having an unpleasant experience in there. Plus there are the two exhibitions and the top floor is open for researchers, so it isn't as if we've closed the whole building.'

'Have any of the staff gone into the reading room since the incident?' asked Luke.

'Not to my knowledge,' said the young man, who wore a purple T-shirt with a *Manchester 1824* logo and *Library Team* printed in white. His name badge, dangling from a lanyard, said *Josh*. 'We've watched the video Jess filmed, and I for one don't want to get hit by a load of books on an escape mission. Apart from any injuries I received, my boss would probably kill me when she saw the forms she'd have to fill in.' He thought for a moment. 'Actually, Ludovic popped in when he arrived today, but he didn't stay long. Not more than five minutes. He said everything seemed fine.'

'Oh.' Not that Luke wanted the library to put on a show for him, but he hoped they hadn't come all this way for a non-event.

Soraya put her hand over the mouthpiece of her phone. 'Still no joy,' she said. 'I'll try the director's office again.' She dialled another extension. A few seconds later, she exclaimed 'At last! You're a hard man to track down. Our visitors are here.' Then she laughed. 'I'll send them to your office – oh?' Another pause. 'In that case, I'll send them there. Bye.' She put the phone down. 'Ludovic would like to meet you outside the Historic Reading Room. It's on the second floor, and the lift and the stairs are both round the corner. Do you need anyone to show you the way?'

'We'll manage,' said Luke, and off they went.

The stairs were an elegant hybrid of old and new: sleek stairs and white walls combined with ancient masonry. 'It's quite something, isn't it?' said Maddy, as they ascended.

'It is,' said Luke, absently. His mind was on what they might find when they reached the second floor. Not just the reading room, but Ludovic. The elusive Assistant Keeper for Manchester had finally been located. He imagined Ludovic would be a tall, angular man, either flamboyantly dressed like Raphael or in fine tailoring. He would probably look down a disapproving nose at them, or peer through wire-rimmed spectacles. Would he have a northern accent? He doubted it.

Not for the first time, Luke wished the Keepers' Guild had a website or intranet where you could read about its members. *Maybe I should suggest it to Jemma.* He visualised his own photograph on the Keepers' Guild web page. He'd probably wear the pale-green shirt. Maybe he could get Maddy to take a few pictures of him here, so he'd have a suitably impressive backdrop...

'Luke,' called Maddy. She had stopped on the landing. 'This is the second floor.'

'Sorry,' he said, and retraced his steps. At least no one else was about and he hadn't been caught woolgathering.

They followed the signs to the Historic Reading Room until they reached an anteroom lined with books. Maddy tried the door, which didn't budge. 'I'll knock.'

'Wait a minute,' said Luke. He tucked his hair behind his ears and stood up straight.

'For heaven's sake,' said Maddy. 'This isn't charm school.' She lifted her hand to rap on the door, but it opened before she could make contact.

Luke found himself looking at empty air. 'Welcome,' said a voice a foot below where he'd expected it.

He looked down and saw a short, bald, squarely built man in a black T-shirt, black jeans and thick black round-framed spectacles. 'Oh, hello,' he said, and held out his hand. 'I'm Luke. You must be Ludovic.'

'That's me.' Ludovic's voice was slightly nasal and strongly Mancunian. He could have been any age from forty to sixty, though given that Keepers didn't age, he could be much, much older. He stepped into the anteroom, closed the door and shook Luke's hand with a crushing grip. 'Who's your glamorous assistant?'

'I'm Madeleine Shenton,' said Maddy. 'Associate Keeper. Pleased to meet you. Shall we get down to business?'

'Hang fire, hang fire,' said Ludovic, holding up both hands. 'I want to check something.' He pointed at Maddy. 'So you're an Associate Keeper. Not an Assistant Keeper?'

'That's right,' said Maddy. Luke hoped Ludovic wouldn't ask them to explain what an Associate Keeper was. He had a feeling that Raphael's lack of definition wouldn't do.

'OK. It's just that, given what's been going on, we were hoping Jemma could find time to pay us a visit. Or Raphael. If he's still about, that is.' Ludovic hooked his thumbs through his belt loops and gazed at Luke.

'Oh, he very much is,' said Luke. 'But Jemma's busy recruiting, and it's a long way for Raphael to come.' He felt as if he was making excuses. Given the way that Ludovic was looking at him, he suspected he knew.

'Mmm,' said Ludovic. 'Now, here's the thing. One of our staff has been terrified in there.' He jerked a thumb at the closed door. 'We've clocked the video, but the member of staff Jess fetched didn't see a thing. Neither did I, when I went in. So we don't know whether what Jess saw was personal to her, or whether the books are on their best behaviour in front of senior staff. If that's the case, they're likely to mess about in front of members of the public. Not good, I'm sure you'll agree.'

'No, not at all,' said Luke.

Ludovic clicked his tongue a few times. 'Tell you what, let's go in and see if it's any different with you two.' He pushed the door open.

'Wow,' breathed Maddy, as she walked into the room and the full grandeur of it hit her: the vaulted ceiling, the soaring arches, the statues and carvings. 'It's even better than the photos.'

'Pretty good, eh?' said Ludovic. 'When it's behaving itself.' His thick dark eyebrows lowered and he sent a scowl round the room.

They walked up and down the two aisles of the reading room, watching for movement on the balconies, peering at the bookcases in the alcoves. Luke braced himself every time he went near one of the two marble statues, in case he experienced the quicksand effect Jemma had described, but he felt nothing. The temperature was normal, the air surprisingly fresh, there was no charge in the atmosphere, no tension. 'Do you feel anything, Maddy?' he murmured.

She shook her head, gazing around her. 'Apart from awe, no.'

'That's pretty conclusive,' said Ludovic. 'Maybe it is just Jess, in which case we can adjust the rota so that she stays out of the reading room. Unless...' He scrutinised Luke, then Maddy. 'Would you mind spending a bit of time in here on your own?'

'Excuse me?' said Maddy.

'Well,' said Ludovic. 'Not to rub it in, but I'm pretty senior in the Keepers' Guild. I'm wondering if whatever's causing bother is keeping quiet because it knows I'll be on to it. It might lose its inhibitions with you two, then we'd have more evidence. Wouldn't we?'

'We came to investigate,' said Maddy. 'Not run risks. Isn't that right, Luke?'

Luke looked around him, playing for time. In his heart of hearts, he agreed with Maddy. But he also wanted to show Ludovic that, junior or not, he had an important contribution to make. 'I agree with Maddy that we shouldn't take unnecessary risks,' he said. 'However, if we do stay in the reading room, we'll learn something, one way or the other.'

'Exactly,' said Ludovic. 'Are you both up for it?'

'No,' said Maddy, decisively.

'Yes,' said Luke, and she gave him a hurt glance. 'Maddy, if you and Ludovic go outside, I'll rejoin you in a few minutes.'

'Good man,' said Ludovic. 'If you'll step this way, Maddy.' His trainers squeaked on the parquet floor. A minute later, the door closed.

Luke swallowed, then opened the knowledge-emergency kit bag, put on the mask and slid his right hand into the leather gauntlet. *One book box can do nothing in here*, he thought. He walked down the left aisle, surveying his surroundings, tensed for any movement.

Nothing happened. The air was still fresh, the room silent apart from his own footsteps.

Maybe it is Jess. Though why a library would target one person—

His footsteps were quickening. Luke looked at his feet in bewilderment. He moved faster and faster, until he was almost running. In desperation, he grabbed the side of a display case and hung on, his feet scrabbling for a hold. He could feel his body being pulled away, his grip loosening.

He pulled off the mask. 'Help!' he yelled.

Why did I agree to this? What was I thinking? His feet were sliding along the floor. He let go of the display case with one hand to try and get a firmer grip, but his arm was pulled into the slipstream. 'Noooooo!'

A door banged open. 'Pack it in!' shouted Ludovic.

Immediately, everything stopped. Luke slumped on the floor.

He heard running feet, then Maddy was crouching beside him. 'Are you all right? Can you stand? What happened?'

'I'm not sure,' murmured Luke. But he was sure of one thing. As an Associate Keeper, he was utterly useless.

CHAPTER 11

Maddy helped Luke to his feet. He was even paler than usual, as pale as the statue of a woman looking down on him. They could have been carved from the same block of marble. 'Lean on me,' she said. 'What happened?'

'Something was pulling me towards it,' said Luke. 'It was – it was the opposite of what Jemma described. She said people were stuck and couldn't move. I felt as if...' He swallowed.

'It's probably best not to talk about it,' said Maddy. 'Especially not in here. We're near a door—'

'Not that way,' said Luke. 'That's closer to whatever it was. Back to the door we came in by.'

Ludovic was standing by the door, arms folded. 'You all right, mate?'

'Not really,' said Luke. 'Something was pulling at me. Something I couldn't see.'

Behind the round glasses, Ludovic's eyes bored into him. 'Was it now.' He uncrossed his arms and walked to meet them. Then he gazed around him and sniffed the air.

'Seems to have gone, whatever it was.'

'Don't you know?' said Luke. 'You told it to pack it in.'

Ludovic scratched his bald head. 'Yeah, I did, didn't I?' He shrugged. 'Obviously it wasn't particularly strong, since it didn't put up much of a fight. Come on.' He turned and walked out.

'Thanks for helping,' muttered Maddy.

'Shhh,' said Luke. 'He'll hear you.'

'I don't care if he does,' Maddy replied. 'You were in danger, and it was his idea. He could at least say sorry.' She deliberately raised her voice for the last sentence.

'You're not helping,' murmured Luke.

'I'm helping you,' said Maddy. She gritted her teeth as she supported Luke to the door. 'Which is more than he's doing.'

Ludovic was waiting in the anteroom for them. 'Yeah, sorry about that,' he said, and Maddy gave Luke a triumphant look. 'I suppose I'm a bit cross. I was hoping this was a Jess problem, but if you've experienced something too then it's bigger.'

'I could have told you that,' said Luke. 'A couple of people have posted on social media about odd experiences they've had in there.'

Ludovic frowned. 'Have they? No one told me. I'll get someone to check. Can't have people badmouthing the library.'

'You mean you can't risk people being hurt,' said Maddy.

'Oh yeah, that goes without saying,' said Ludovic. He paused, studying them both. 'Well, that was interesting, though it wasn't the result I wanted. Why don't you two go for a coffee before you head back? I'll drop Jemma an email, let her know you had a good go.'

'Wait a minute,' said Maddy. 'Head back? We've only just got here.'

'Yeah, but to be honest, I doubt you can do much. Whatever's in there seems wily, seeing as it never shows itself to me. So I reckon it's gonna take someone even more senior, like Jemma or Raphael, to fix it.'

'Coffee's a good idea,' murmured Luke. He was swaying slightly, and Maddy didn't dare let go of him.

Ludovic gave him a robust pat on the shoulder. 'Yeah, you definitely need something. Stick a couple of sugars in it, too. You look like you're in shock.' He nodded. 'Give it a year or two, you'll probably be able to take this stuff in your stride. Gotta work up to it, you see.'

He glanced at his watch, a chunky silver number. 'I'd better get going: I want to pop into Stretford Library. Safe journey home.' He strode off with the air of someone who has to be everywhere at once. His stride was slightly too long for his height, so that his head bobbed as he moved. He turned right and was lost to sight.

'We'll take the lift,' said Maddy.

'Good idea,' said Luke. 'I wouldn't trust myself on the stairs.'

Maddy gave Luke a hug in the lift. He put his arms round her too, but it felt more a token gesture than a demonstration of affection. 'Do you feel any better?' she asked.

'A bit. Not much.'

Maddy tried to keep her face neutral, though inside she was scowling. How dare Ludovic send Luke into that room without backup, then dismiss them? 'If I let go of you, will you be OK?'

Luke made a face. 'Maybe.'

Soon they were on the ground floor. 'Why don't you head to the entrance,' said Maddy. 'I'll sign us both out and ask them to recommend a coffee shop.' Apart from anything else, she hoped that engaging the reception staff in a conversation would distract them from any wobbliness on Luke's part.

'That was quick,' said Soraya, as Maddy wrote the time on the signing-out sheet.

'We'll have a coffee and regroup,' said Maddy. 'Where would you recommend?'

'I like Federal Coffee,' said Josh. 'Out of here, turn right, about three minutes' walk. It's a dark little place—'

'Perfect,' said Maddy. 'We'll get a brew, talk things over and maybe see you later.'

'Did anything—'

'Sorry, just got to catch Luke. Bye!' Maddy hurried after Luke, hoping Ludovic would be too busy to update the staff on the latest occurrence in the reading room.

Luke was waiting outside, studying a restaurant called Sexy Fish. 'OK, let's go,' said Maddy. She put an arm round his waist and draped his arm over her shoulders.

At Federal Coffee, Luke sat at a table in the gloom while Maddy went to the counter. 'Can I have an Americano and a tea, please?' She scanned the menu. 'And a steak sandwich, as rare as you can.' Hopefully that would help a little.

Luke managed a shaky smile when she told him about the sandwich. 'Thanks, Maddy.'

'Put sugar in your coffee when it arrives,' said Maddy. 'Much as I hate to agree with Ludovic, you may be in shock.'

Luke's lip curled. 'I suppose.'

Three minutes later he poured sugar in his drink and took an experimental sip. 'Ugh.'

'I should have gone in there with you,' said Maddy.

'What? No!' Luke stared at her. 'I didn't want to say anything in front of Ludovic, but it was really scary. I had no idea what to do. It was fine, and then it wasn't.'

'I bet nothing would have happened if we'd been in there together,' said Maddy. 'From what you've told me, stuff only happens in there when people are alone.'

'That wouldn't have told us anything,' said Luke. 'In fact, it would have misled Ludovic into believing Jess is the problem.'

'We have to talk to Jess.' Maddy sipped her own drink and set it down. 'And speak to Jemma, preferably before Ludovic does.'

Luke held his mug in both hands. He seemed to need the warmth. 'Do we have to?'

'Yes, of course we do. He'll probably say we're a pair of amateurs.'

'We are,' said Luke. 'I mean, it was horrible, but Ludovic stopped it just like that, without knowing what it was.' He studied the table. 'I think he's right, and it does require someone more senior. Even though there isn't anyone.'

'What do you mean? Jemma or Raphael could come. Gertrude would probably get them here and back in half a day.'

'No way,' said Luke. 'Absolutely not.'

Maddy folded her arms. 'Why not? Jemma's recruited her Assistant Keeper, so she can leave Hermione in charge.'

Luke bit his lip. 'That isn't it.'

'So what is? What's the big secret?'

He seemed to be looking everywhere but at her. 'I'm not supposed to say. Jemma can't get involved in any book emergency stuff right now.' He met her eyes. 'Or for the next . . . let's say seven or eight months, at least.'

'So long?' The penny dropped as Luke's sandwich arrived. 'Oh my gosh.' Maddy put a hand over her mouth as if she had told the secret.

'Exactly. And Raphael's semi-retired. We can't send either of them into it.'

'So it really is up to us.' Maddy took a long drink of tea.

'Is it?' Luke picked up his sandwich and took a bite. Blood dripped onto the plate. 'This is nice,' he said, once he'd swallowed. 'I'd offer you the other half, but...'

Maddy waved the offer away. 'So what do we do?'

Luke wiped his fingers on his napkin. 'If we don't hang around, we could probably be at the bookshop by lunchtime.'

'What?'

Luke shrugged. 'I can't do anything, you can't do

94

anything. What's the point of staying?'

'Wasn't this meant to be your big chance to prove yourself?'

'Which I've completely failed to do,' said Luke. 'Thanks for mentioning.'

'No, you haven't. We've barely started.'

'What, so I'm supposed to go in that library again after what happened? Knowing the staff are probably laughing behind my back and waiting to see what the reading room does to me next time? No, thank you. I'll go home and put all the Keeper nonsense out of my head. It clearly isn't meant to be.'

'You had one go. One.' Maddy drank more tea while she wondered how to say what she wanted to without hurting Luke's feelings. 'How did you feel when you were in the room?'

'I told you. It was fine, then it wasn't. I was being pulled across the room. I couldn't keep my footing. I managed to grab a display case. That was the only thing that kept me from...'

'From what?'

'I don't know. It was horrible. I felt powerless. I'd already realised one book box was no use in a room full of volatile books.'

'So you felt as if you weren't properly equipped?'

Luke considered. 'Maybe. It was just so sudden. And I knew what those other people had experienced.'

'Mmm. Do you think . . . not that you imagined it, but—'

'Of course I didn't imagine it! You saw me. I was

hanging on for my life. You can't imagine that.'

'OK, OK,' Maddy soothed, though she found Luke's defensiveness slightly irritating. 'I'm trying to work out something complicated and it isn't easy. Like I said, I don't think you imagined it. Maybe your apprehension, your realisation that you weren't adequately equipped and your knowledge of other people's experiences worked together to magnify what happened.'

Luke thought this over. 'Do you mean that what I was feeling made it worse? Or do you mean that the room – or the thing in the room – knew what I was thinking? If that's it, I'm definitely not going back in there.'

Maddy drained her cup. 'I need more tea. Do you want anything?'

'I wouldn't mind another coffee,' said Luke, rather sulkily.

There was a queue at the counter. Normally Maddy hated queues, but she was relieved to have some breathing space. Occasionally she glanced at Luke, who was staring into the middle distance, more wraithlike than ever. *We can't give up*, she thought. *How ironic. First I didn't want Luke to come here, then I didn't want to come with him, and now I'm the one arguing that we should stay.* Indeed, she was surprised at her own determination.

She scanned the drinks options. *I might have a chai latte. Those bagels look nice.*

She sighed. *Maybe this is what love is*, she thought. *Trying to get the other person to do the right thing, even when you'd rather they didn't.*

Come off it. You're not being unselfish. If anything, it's

96

the opposite. You don't want to be beaten, you want to prove Ludovic wrong, and most of all, you want to prowl around that library.

The queue shuffled forward.

Yes, I do. I probably won't get the chance again.

She looked at the artwork on the walls, the other customers, what was going on outside. Anything rather than dwell on how she would persuade Luke.

As she walked to the table, she decided to stick to the facts and get it over with. 'OK, here's the thing,' she said, as she sat down. 'We have to speak to Jess, and we probably have more chance of doing that now Ludovic's not around. From the sound of it, he's keeping her shut away on the top floor.'

'Like Bertha in *Jane Eyre*,' said Luke.

'Exactly. That didn't go well, did it? We need to hear her story. We need to find out exactly what happened and how she felt, so we can compare her experience with yours.'

'OK… That's not too bad.' Luke finished his coffee and gazed at her. 'I'm sorry I lashed out,' he said. 'I think I'm tired.'

'I think so too.' He had dark shadows under his eyes and his cheeks looked hollow. 'Tell you what, when we're done, why don't you have a nap in Gertrude?'

'That's a good idea. We can rest a bit, go and talk to Jess, then head home.'

Maddy just managed to stop herself rolling her eyes. 'Or . . . you could rest while I send a message to Jemma, then we talk to Jess, explore the rest of the library, drive to

97

the Airbnb and go out for dinner.'

Luke frowned slightly. 'You mean stay?'

'Why not?' said Maddy, with studied casualness. 'Jemma's already paid for the Airbnb. It's ridiculous not to enjoy it when we've come all this way. Also, I'm not sure I fancy driving to Manchester and back in one day.'

'I thought Gertrude did most of the work.'

'I'm the one behind the wheel,' said Maddy. 'And we had an early start.'

'That's true.' Luke yawned. 'That could be why I'm tired.' He jumped and sat up straight as a server arrived with their drinks.

'I think you're right,' said Maddy. *Hopefully you'll feel more positive about things when you wake*, she thought. *Because I want a proper look at that library.*

CHAPTER 12

Despite two large coffees, Luke was yawning when they climbed into Gertrude. As the van was mostly used as a book-expedition vehicle, she was fitted with a long bench on either side and the rest of the space was left open for crates and boxes. Their luggage didn't even fill the space beneath the benches.

Maddy drew the curtains at the little windows for privacy while Luke grabbed a cushion for a pillow and stretched out on the left-hand bench. 'Sorry to be a party pooper,' he said. 'I'll be more use if I have a power nap.'

'It's fine,' said Maddy. 'I'll text Jemma, then read, or go through the wedding list, or something. Do you want me to wake you at a particular time?'

'Say an hour? We could eat our lunch and discuss next steps.'

'Are you sure that's long enough?'

Luke considered, eyes closed. 'I'd have thought so. I mean...' He yawned. 'I wasn't driving, and what happened didn't take very long. Maybe we've both got recovery powers…'

I hope so, thought Maddy.

'Yeah…' His eyelids fluttered and his breathing slowed.

I wish I could do that, thought Maddy. She often found it hard to get to sleep at night. Thoughts ran round her head: things she could have done better, things she had left undone, things she must remember to do tomorrow.

And she had found, over the last three years or so, that she was waking earlier. She had always been a morning person, which annoyed her, since it was hardly appropriate for the woman of Gothic mystery she would love to be. Now, though, it was normal for her to wake at five or earlier, instantly wide awake and with no hope of getting back to sleep.

She watched Luke sleep for a while, until his calm expression and regular breathing became infuriating, then took out her phone and began a message to Jemma.

Hi, she wrote, and racked her brains for how to put what she wanted to say. *We've arrived at the library. We met Ludovic briefly and Luke had a small run-in with the reading room. So something's definitely not right there. Luke seems fine but he's a bit tired. He's having a nap in Gertrude and then we'll chat to the staff. Hope all is well in London. Say hi to the cats for me. Maddy x*

She considered deleting the *x*, decided to leave it and pressed *Send*. It felt very odd that she knew about Jemma's pregnancy but could say nothing. At some point, presumably, it would become obvious and Jemma would make an announcement. That would be a relief, as Maddy had a distinct feeling that Jemma would see that she knew the minute she set eyes on her.

Maddy opened Pinterest, where she had a secret board devoted to wedding matters. She scrolled through the pins, but she wasn't in the mood.

The phone buzzed.

Hi Maddy, thanks for messaging. Impressed you managed to actually meet Ludovic. Tell Luke to rest as much as he needs and be careful. Ben rang in sick so Raphael is helping out. Keep in touch, Jemma x

Maddy put the phone on the bench and looked around the van. She wasn't at all tired. She checked the time: Luke had been asleep for less than ten minutes.

What am I going to do, sit and twitch for an hour?

An idea came to her and she crouched beside Luke. 'I might pop out for a bit,' she whispered. 'I'll take my phone.'

'OK,' murmured Luke.

'I won't be long. Love you.'

'Fussawummer...'

Maddy undid her plait and shook out her hair, then opened the suitcase and found the raincoat she'd packed just in case. Luke had put in a pair of sunglasses, which she borrowed. *That should do it*, she thought. *They won't make everyone sign in.* Two minutes later, she got down from the van and gently closed the door.

It felt strange being on her own in a city she'd never visited. She remembered when she had had to wear a disguise in London, when they were on the run, and shivered. This was different. *I'm in my own clothes and no one's chasing me. I'm choosing to change my appearance so that I can explore the library in peace.*

Maddy walked into reception, browsed the gift shop then moved to the stairwell. This time she climbed to the first floor, which promised exhibitions. A brightly lit ramp led to a sort of cloister, and she went to investigate.

I could imagine myself living here, she thought as she gazed at the windows, made of tiny round leaded panes, then walked round the exhibition galleries. One exhibition was about the items stored in the library, and one of the first things Maddy saw was a Gutenberg Bible, printed in heavy Gothic black-letter script with red accents. She roamed happily from case to case, gazing at illustrations, plans and reproductions of rare books. Even without the exhibitions, the book-lined rooms would have been fascinating in their own right.

The corridor ran around the outside of the exhibition rooms and Maddy came to a set of stone steps which led down to a square space. An identical flight rose on the other side, and above her were more windows, stone arches supporting a beautiful staircase, and all manner of interesting carvings and mouldings.

On the opposite landing, a guide was holding forth to a group. Maddy estimated there must be fifteen of them. Casually she made her way over, looking about like a tourist, until she was standing at the rear of the group.

'You'll agree that it's a remarkable structure,' said the guide, a tall, white-haired man in a bright red waistcoat. His name badge said *Paul*. 'Now we'll go to the Historic Reading Room. It's actually closed today, but I have special permission for us to see it and a member of staff will accompany us. If you'll follow me.' He took the group to the landing, then to a wider staircase with an iron handrail in the middle.

Maddy followed. At first she hung back, worried that if she stayed too close someone in the group might detect an interloper in their midst. But after some observation, she realised the group wasn't moving as one. People tended to walk singly or in pairs, so presumably they were random people on a tour rather than a cohesive group.

She was lagging, and quickened her pace. The last thing she wanted was to miss another opportunity to see inside the reading room.

The stairs curved round to a landing, with a curved balustrade at the top, and an arched doorway. In front of it stood a blonde, round-faced, middle-aged woman wearing the uniform T-shirt.

Paul walked over and stood beside her. 'Yvonne has kindly agreed to allow us access to the reading room. Before we go in, can I ask that you keep to the main area. Various doors are closed in the reading room and we ask you to respect that. Similarly, please keep away from areas marked private. You may take photographs for personal use, but for the sake of the valuable items within, please do not use a flash and observe any no-photography signs.' He beamed at the group. 'In we go!'

Yvonne opened one door and held it as the group trickled in.

Paul strode towards the first display case and took up position with his back to it. 'Gather round,' he said.

The group straggled over. Yvonne seemed to be

counting heads. Then she closed the door and stood foursquare like a sentry.

'So, welcome to the Historic Reading Room. The statue in front of you is of Enriqueta Rylands. Now, the name of the library might suggest that it was founded by John Rylands, but in fact the library was built by Enriqueta, his widow. It opened on New Year's Day 1900, and it was meant for the people of Manchester. Not just the rich people: anyone who wanted to learn.'

Maddy studied the statue. Enriqueta Rylands was rendered in pale marble and gazed straight ahead. Maddy followed her gaze. She had thought it would lead to the statue of a man at the other end of the room, but actually Enriqueta was gazing into the distance: perhaps into a future only she could see. *She must have been very determined*, Maddy thought. *Imagine overseeing this.*

She looked around her: at the counter, the door marked *LIBRARIAN*, what must be the stacks in the corner, the thousands of books waiting in display cases. Her eyes narrowed, but there was no noise, no movement. The air was fresh, too. *It's because lots of us are here*, she thought. *Lots of witnesses.*

I wonder what the library is trying to do. Or is it the library causing problems? Could it be something else? She longed to walk up and down, to peer into corners and run her hands over the stonework, but everyone was listening to the guide, who was talking about the statues being in pairs. She felt guilty for not paying attention, then reasoned that she could learn the history of the library on the internet later.

She cast her mind back to the events of a few months ago, when first the bookshops, then their staff had been in danger. Indeed, all of London had been in danger. That was the problem. She had been busy keeping the shops running, and as far as possible, not thinking too much about what was going on. She had worried about everyone, and Luke in particular, but much of the detail was hazy now. In fact, she wasn't sure it had ever been clear.

She huffed in annoyance and a man looked round reproachfully. The lens of his large camera glared at her too.

'Sorry,' whispered Maddy.

He gave her a tight smile and faced the front.

What could I have done? she thought. *The others – most of the others – have powers. I don't. I'm...* The word *powerless* seemed too much. *I'm just me.*

But now I'm an Associate Keeper, could that change?

'So this really is a library of the people and a library for the ages,' said Paul the guide. He glanced at Yvonne, who tapped her watch and held up a hand, fingers spread. 'OK, you have five minutes, then we'll move on. Please remember what I said about keeping to the public areas.'

Slowly people spread out, reading the information in the display cases, craning to look at the figures above their heads, taking pictures of the room, the great window, each other. Maddy walked down the left-hand aisle to the study tables in the centre, straining to feel, to perceive. *How do Jemma and Raphael summon their powers?*

She thought of the one occasion when she had been present as Luke transformed. He had asked her not to watch as he stripped off.

'How will I know when you're . . . done?' she had asked.

'You'll know,' he said.

She had turned her back, and for no reason that she was sure of, closed her eyes. There had been rustling as his clothes dropped to the ground. A few seconds later she had almost been blown over by the gust of wind as a colony of bats flew on their mission. How had Luke done it?

Then there was the glamour. Both Luke and Em seemed able to switch it on – or off – at will. *Maybe it happens when it needs to*, she thought. In all honesty, she had never wanted to have any magical ability of her own. She had been mistrustful and suspicious of magic, even. Books had always been enough for her.

'If you can start making your way over...' called the guide.

Maddy realised she was frowning in her attempt to feel something. Her fists were clenched at her sides. *Let go*, she told herself.

She took a deep breath and did her best to think of nothing. It was incredibly difficult. *I hate not being in control.*

Maddy let that thought go, too. She took a step forward, then another.

As she walked, the skin between her shoulder blades tingled, like the beginning of an itch. Maddy looked around, hoping something would make it stronger. It didn't vary. But now she was sure it was real.

As Maddy walked towards the group forming at the

door, the place where the itch was throbbed slightly, as if it was pulsing. Something was in her mind, but it was so vague and insubstantial that she couldn't catch it.

Yvonne counted the heads then murmured to Paul. 'Thank you, everyone,' he said. 'Now we'll visit the printing press.'

Yvonne opened the door. Maddy could see her lips moving as she counted them out, and her stance was more relaxed.

The group meandered along behind Paul. Maddy considered visiting the printing press, but she was too excited to stand still. *I felt something*, she thought, as she peeled away from the group and hurried downstairs. *I know I did.*

CHAPTER 13

Luke walked down the dark street. To all appearances, he was sauntering casually: one more person heading home after a trip to the pub or a late evening at work. His pace, however, was faster than one might have expected. It was the pace of a man who wants to catch up with someone.

That someone was a few metres ahead, walking quickly, sometimes hidden in shadows, sometimes illuminated by a street lamp. They hurried on and never looked back.

Gradually, Luke increased his pace. He was perhaps two metres behind now—

What's this? Someone had taken hold of his shoulder. He wriggled free, but they did it again.

'Luke… Luke, wake up.'

He opened his eyes and saw Maddy. 'Oh.' He blinked, giving himself time to adjust to the real world. 'Hello.' *Where am I?*

'Were you dreaming?' she asked.

'I was, yes.' *This isn't my bed.* Slowly, he got himself

into a sitting position, realising as he did so that they were in Gertrude. *Oh yes*, he thought. *Manchester.*

'Was it a hunting dream?'

Oh God. 'Yeah. You woke me before I caught them.'

'Good.' Maddy hated the hunting dreams. He didn't know what he said or did when he was having one, but clearly it was too much for her. He'd explained that there was nothing he could do about it, that even non-practising vampires had them from time to time. 'Do you need anything?' she asked. 'I've got a bottle of water and there's tea in the flask.'

'Water would be good.' He ran his tongue over his dry lips. Then he looked at Maddy properly. 'Hang on. Why is your hair down? And why have you put a coat on? It's not cold.'

'I'll get the water,' said Maddy.

How long have I been asleep? He checked his watch. 'I thought you wanted to let me sleep longer than an hour.'

Maddy put the bottle in his hand. 'I've got something to tell you. Then we must go to the library and talk to the staff.'

'What about lunch?'

'Of course. After I've told you.'

Luke took a long drink. The water cleared the fur from his mouth. That was the thing with hunting dreams: whether you caught your prey or not, you always woke feeling bloated and dirty. 'So, what have you been up to? You said you were going out for a bit.'

'I went to the library.'

Luke's eyebrows shot up. 'On your own? You didn't…'

109

Maddy nodded, a little smile on her face. 'I got into the reading room. With a group of people, not on my own,' she added, hastily. 'And I felt something.'

'You felt something?' For a moment he was back in the reading room, gripping the display case and feeling his fingers slip as he tried not to get sucked into whatever was in there. But Maddy didn't seem distressed at all. 'What sort of something?' he asked, and made an effort to slow his breathing. 'I drank that water a bit too fast,' he said.

'It wasn't much,' said Maddy. 'I didn't have a vision, or anything. It was . . . a feeling. Just as I was walking towards the exit. A sort of tingle. I have no idea what it was or what it meant, but it was definitely there.'

'Right,' said Luke. 'How did you get into the reading room? It's out of bounds.'

'I sneaked in on the back of a guided tour. The hair and the coat were so that the staff didn't recognise me and start asking questions: where you'd got to, what we're planning to do next. That sort of thing.'

'OK.' Luke drank more water while he collected his thoughts. It was easy for him to accept that Maddy had felt something in the reading room: he had had quite the experience when he'd been there alone. But as far as he knew, no one had experienced anything when there were witnesses. *Unless Maddy's so desperate to get in on the action that she's... Not made it up, but imagined a thing that perhaps wasn't there.* 'So you got changed and went back in the library. Then what?'

'The staff didn't notice me, so the disguise must have worked,' said Maddy.

The disguise. Maddy had been so uncomfortable when she had had to disguise herself a few months ago. Now she was voluntarily sneaking about. 'OK. And…?'

'I walked around the library for a bit. It really is absolutely beautiful. I could see myself living there.'

'I'm sure you could.'

'I saw a group, and the guide was saying they had special permission to go in the reading room. So I tagged along.'

'You infiltrated a guided tour?' He smiled, but he felt far from smiling. Maddy never did anything sneaky. She had perhaps the best-developed conscience of anyone he had ever met. If a customer had dropped five pence, she would have sprinted after them with it. 'That isn't like you.'

Maddy shrugged. 'It was an opportunity. You'd have done the same.'

'I probably would.' He mused. Maddy had acted out of character before. Both times, it had been when someone was manipulating her. Discovering what had happened had made her even more suspicious of any form of magic. Maddy was – what was the word? Susceptible. Who could have got to her this time?

'OK, so you went to the reading room.'

'We weren't in there long. A member of staff was there with us, and when the guide finished talking she gave us five minutes to look around. I was taking it all in when the guide called us. I wondered if I might have magical powers while I'm in the Keepers' Guild, and I sort of – let go.'

Luke stared at her. 'You never let go.'

'Well, I did. That's when I felt it. We had to leave, so I came to see if you'd woken up.'

'Right. I bet you're hungry after all that. Let's eat. Oh, and if we're going back to the library, you should probably take the coat off and plait your hair.'

'Yes, sir.' Maddy saluted, then rummaged in the suitcase.

Luke watched her brush and plait, in the calm, efficient way she always did. *What's going on? Who's got to her?*

Has someone got into her?

***

After demolishing their packed lunch, they walked to the library and went to the desk. 'Hello again,' said Josh. 'I'm afraid Ludovic's gone, if you wanted to speak to him. Can't say when he'll be back.' His expression said *if ever.*

'That's fine,' said Luke. 'Could we speak to Jess?'

'Ah. Normally that wouldn't be a problem, but Jess is out this afternoon. She's at the other John Rylands: the university library. She's representing us at a network meeting.'

'Right,' said Luke. 'Will she be here tomorrow?'

'Oh yes,' said Josh.

'Is there anyone else who could help us in the meantime?'

Josh thought. 'We've all seen the video she took, but I imagine you've watched that, too. The best person is probably Yvonne, Jess's boss. She's the first person Jess told and she went to the reading room with her, so she's as close as we've got to a firsthand account.' He consulted his monitor. 'According to this, she's in Reader Services on the top floor. I'll give her a ring and let her know you're coming.'

'Thank you,' said Maddy, and steered Luke away from the desk. 'Oops,' she murmured, with a little smile on her face.

'What do you mean, oops?'

'When I sneaked into the reading room with that tour, Yvonne was the member of staff on duty,' said Maddy. 'Oh well. If she recognises me, I'll say I got too hot and my hair was annoying me.'

'Uh-huh.' Luke went to examine the book display. Uneasiness knotted his stomach. *Normally you'd be racked with guilt over something like this*, he thought. *Maybe that'll happen when you come face to face with her.* He felt rather mean for hoping it did. This new, confident Maddy was making him nervous.

'Let's take the lift,' said Maddy, and strode towards the stairwell.

'How do we play this?' she asked, once the lift was moving.

'I assume we'll ask her how Jess seemed, what she said and whether she felt anything when they went back in. We can cross reference it with Jess tomorrow.'

'Do we ask her anything about the library? Odd happenings, disturbances, rows between staff?'

'Oh yes, that goes without saying,' said Luke.

'Just wanted to be sure.' Was she smirking?

'As you've already encountered Yvonne, it's probably best if I ask the questions,' he said. 'That leaves you free to take notes.'

113

'I hope you'll take notes too,' said Maddy, with her usual precision. 'We don't want to miss anything.'

'I meant you'll be able to listen more. I'll be thinking of my next question.'

'OK, whatever.'

The lift came to a halt and the door slid open. Luke was relieved to escape.

The public face of Reader Services was a wooden lobby with a wide glass window. Through it they could see a square office with glass walls, against which were propped thank-you cards. A woman with curly blonde hair was sitting inside. She looked up when they opened the outer door.

'That's Yvonne,' Maddy whispered.

Yvonne got up and came to the window. 'Are you the book detectives?' she asked. 'I'm afraid your bird's flown the coop for the day, but I'll do what I can.'

She walked round and opened the inner door. 'Come on in. We'll have to keep it down, because we've got researchers in.' She nodded at another large window which gave onto a room with a big table surrounded by chairs. Two people sat opposite each other, engrossed in large volumes supported by padded book rests.

'They're here a lot,' Yvonne mouthed. 'I have no idea what they're researching, or if they'll ever finish. Anyway. Take a seat. Do you want a brew?'

'No, we're fine, thanks,' said Luke. 'By the way, I'm Luke and this is Maddy.' He watched Yvonne closely for any sign of recognition, but there was none. In one way that was a relief, but it didn't say much for her powers of observation.

They sat and Maddy took out a notebook. Luke leaned forward. 'Could you tell us about what happened on the day when Jess had her . . . experience in the reading room.'

'Oh yes,' said Yvonne. 'I was here that day, too. Jess came through the door like a tornado, saying "The books in the reading room have gone weird!"'

Luke saw Maddy write a note. 'Then what happened?' he asked.

Yvonne laughed. 'At first I assumed it was something and nothing. Jess reads fantasy novels and watches all sorts. Horror, vampires, werewolves, you name it.' Luke concentrated on appearing as unvampirical as he could. 'This place is perfect for her. Then she showed me the video. I know they can fake stuff these days, but the video was time-stamped two minutes before. So I made her a strong cup of tea with lots of sugar and asked her what exactly had happened. She said she'd been on the gallery shelving, heard thumping, looked down, and the books were banging the glass as if they wanted to get out. Take it from me, that's not normal.'

Luke glanced at Maddy. 'Have you got that?'

'Yes, thank you,' said Maddy, giving him a glance that could have soured milk. 'Do go on,' she said to Yvonne.

'So I said I'd come down. We can't have books damaging themselves, not here. Jess said "Do I have to go in?" So I said "You don't have to, but it might help. You'll be able to see if it's getting worse or not. And we'll have to lock the reading room, anyway. We can't have people getting involved with shenanigans like that."'

'So you went together,' said Luke.

'Yes. I made her finish her tea and eat a couple of biscuits first. She said she felt a bit better then. We went down and Jess hung back, so I said I'd go first. Not a sausage.'

'Nothing at all?'

'No. So I called to Jess that it was safe to go in and eventually she put her head round the door. She had a funny expression on her face. As if she was glad, but also a little bit sorry. She came in and stood near the door. "But I saw them and I heard them," she said. "I know you did," I said. "I watched the video."'

'Then what happened?' asked Maddy.

'She said "If I hadn't taken that video, you wouldn't believe me, would you?" She sounded a bit resentful, to be honest. So I said "It's good that you did, isn't it?"' Yvonne leaned forward confidentially. 'Jess gets touchy about things. I didn't want to upset her more than she already was. I think she was disappointed.'

'In what way?' Luke asked.

'Well, she's into fantasy stuff but she looked terrified when she came up. I reckon she was disappointed in herself. When she came down with me and it had all gone...' She frowned, as if trying to recall something that had slipped her mind. 'Anyway, I got her to walk around the reading room with me and nothing happened.'

'Did either of you notice anything?' asked Luke. 'A change in the atmosphere, a funny smell, anything like that?'

'It was the same as always.'

116

'How is Jess?' asked Maddy.

Yvonne considered. 'She's all right. She doesn't talk about it, just gets on with things. Ludovic's keeping her out of the reading room and away from the public.' She snorted good-humouredly. 'I was surprised when he turned up. Nice enough bloke, but always on his way somewhere. Never stands still for long. To be fair, until recently our director's been very hands-on. Now he's on this sabbatical, writing a book, we haven't heard a peep.' She grinned. 'In a way, it's a relief. There's being hands-on, then there's being into everything.'

'How long has he been on sabbatical?'

'Not long,' said Yvonne. 'A few weeks, maybe two months.'

'Great,' said Luke. 'Thank you for your help, Yvonne.'

'Before we finish,' said Maddy, 'do the staff generally get on with each other?'

'Oh yes,' Yvonne said comfortably. 'We're a good team.'

'Excellent,' said Luke. 'OK, we'll leave it there.' He stood up to leave no room for doubt. 'We'll come back tomorrow and meet with Jess.'

'She'll probably say the same as I did,' said Yvonne. 'In her own way.' Her expression was amused.

They left Reader Services and summoned the lift. 'What do you think?' asked Maddy, as they glided down.

'I think we should take a stroll around the library, so that I've seen as much of it as *you* have, then let the staff know we'll be in tomorrow and head to the Airbnb. We can talk things over in private there.'

117

'So we *will* stay on and investigate.' Maddy's eyes gleamed.

'Oh yes,' said Luke. 'Books don't behave like that for no reason. I want to get to the bottom of it.'

'So do I,' said Maddy, as the lift eased gently to a stop.

CHAPTER 14

'Gosh, I'm full,' said Maddy, as Luke unlocked the door of the apartment. 'That was a lovely curry. Yours looked nice, too.'

'It was,' said Luke. 'Though enormous.'

They had gone to Namaste Nepal, a restaurant a short walk from their Airbnb apartment, which was in a place called Didsbury in South Manchester. Luke hadn't been sure what to expect: the food descriptions sounded great but the prices were suspiciously reasonable. His eyes boggled when he was served dil-khush masala, a huge chicken breast stuffed with lamb mince, and it was every bit as delicious as the description on the menu.

Maddy had eaten well, too, hoovering up a vegetable pilau. That was good, as they both needed their strength, but it was unusual for her to eat a heavy evening meal. *We've been up since early morning and walking round a big library*, Luke told himself. *Of course we're both hungry.*

That afternoon, Maddy had shown him around the

library – except the reading room – telling him all she could remember of what the guide had said. Once, they met Soraya in an exhibition room. 'Still here?' she said.

'We're getting a feel for the rest of the library,' said Maddy. 'We'll head off soon, but we'll be back tomorrow morning.'

'Superb,' said Soraya.

Eventually, they left the library and returned to Gertrude, who looked perfectly at home in her personal parking space. 'Time to go,' said Maddy. She unlocked the van and climbed up to the driver's seat, then started the engine. 'Do you have the postcode for the Airbnb, Luke?'

'Hang on a minute,' said Luke. 'Let me get in.' He opened the passenger door and took his time making himself comfortable and putting on his seatbelt. Only then did he take out his phone. 'Jemma texted me the address.'

Maddy undid the front of Gertrude's clock to reveal the small round satnav screen and he read the address.

'Did you get that, Gertrude?' asked Maddy.

Slowly, a green arrow appeared on the screen. 'That's a yes.' Maddy put on her own seatbelt. 'Off we go.'

They squeezed along the narrow road, then negotiated various back streets until they were on Deansgate.

'I thought you'd be more nervous,' said Luke, 'driving in a city you don't know.'

Maddy shrugged. 'Gertrude's doing the work. My job is to look like I am.' She changed gear, and a few minutes later they were going down Princess Road again.

The Airbnb turned out to be an apartment in a large Victorian house sitting on a wide, tree-lined road. 'This is definitely the right place, isn't it?' said Luke

'According to Gertrude,' said Maddy. 'It's the right house number. Let's go and see.'

Along with the postcode and house number, Jemma had sent the passcode for a lockbox. Luke attempted to hold his phone and open the box, but it was easier for Maddy's small fingers to perform the manoeuvres to get the keys. 'This is exciting,' she said, as she closed the lockbox and spun the barrels of the combination lock.

'Um, I suppose it is. You go first, and then you can invite me in.'

'Oh yes, of course.'

Inside was a small vestibule, then an imposing high-ceilinged hall with a grand, steep staircase. They ascended, Luke glad that they had travelled reasonably light as he heaved the case upstairs.

The door of the apartment opened into a large lounge with a big squashy leather sofa, a kitchenette to one side and a steel and glass dining table and chairs.

'Lovely,' said Maddy, and opened the other door. She gasped. 'Come and see!'

Luke walked over and found himself looking at a four-poster bed. A small one, admittedly, but a four poster nonetheless.

'Wow!' Maddy walked into the bedroom, sat on the bed and bounced gently.

Luke opened the door to the ensuite and found an old-fashioned bathroom complete with clawfoot tub. He imagined sharing it with Maddy later, or perhaps the next morning, and a grin spread over his face.

Now they had eaten and were back in the apartment, and he couldn't have felt less like sleep. *Maybe we should have gone for a drink.* But they had agreed not to discuss the case in public. Also, they'd both had a drink at the restaurant. *We must keep a clear head*, he thought.

'Why don't I make us a hot drink and we can discuss the case,' said Maddy. 'We've seen and heard a lot today. If we get it all straight in our heads, we can hit the ground running tomorrow.'

Hit the ground running. What is this, a TV drama? Luke just managed to stop himself rolling his eyes. *What's got into her?* he thought, not for the first time that day. 'That's a good idea,' he said. 'I'd love a tea.'

'On it.' Maddy went to the kitchenette and filled the kettle.

Luke had observed her ever since his suspicions had been aroused earlier. Usually, Maddy was a hesitant, tentative person – she certainly had been when she had climbed into Gertrude early that morning. But as the day had worn on, she had become quick, decisive and independent. She had even gone to the library without him.

In the library, he'd worried that Maddy had been manipulated or possessed by someone. Now, watching her hum as she found a teapot and got out the milk, that didn't seem right.

She isn't possessed, Luke thought. *She's different.* He wasn't sure how he felt about that.

Maddy warmed the pot, put the lid on, then looked over her shoulder. 'Where shall we start?'

'I was wondering about the wedding.'

Her eyes widened. 'The wedding?'

'Yes.' *Why did I say that?* 'Erm, how are the arrangements going? Now that I'm legal.'

'Oh. I see. Hang on a minute, I'll get the tea going.' Maddy dropped teabags in the pot, made the tea and popped on a cheerful red and yellow striped tea cosy. Then she came and sat beside him on the sofa. 'I'd already emailed the registrar to reserve the date we wanted, and I'd made a provisional booking with the venue, as there isn't a cancellation charge. So we can confirm those and get on with the invitations as soon as we're back in London.'

'Right. Wow.'

Maddy put a hand on his arm. 'I'm sorry, I did mean to tell you, but with everything else going on it slipped my mind.'

'Yes, I can see how it would.' Luke gazed at Maddy. *You've been obsessed with the wedding for ages, and you forgot to tell me you'd practically booked it. Because this case distracted you.* He took Maddy in his arms and held her tight. *I feel as if you're slipping away from me.* 'Maybe we should send save-the-date emails,' he said, into her hair. 'We could do that here. Do you have a guest list?'

She pulled back to look at him, beaming. 'Of course I do! Let me pour the tea and I'll get the laptop.' Then her body tensed. 'What do we do about Brian?'

'I said I'd write, didn't I, care of Burns Books.' He released Maddy, who got up and went to the kitchenette. 'I wonder if there's any writing paper.'

Luke stood and went to the sideboard. In the middle drawer, underneath various instruction manuals, a sewing kit and a frisbee, he found a writing set with paper and envelopes. 'Bingo.' He got a pen, sat down at the dining table, and thought.

Dear Brian, he wrote, then tapped his teeth with the biro.

Maddy put two mugs on the table, fetched the laptop and sat opposite him. When she opened the lid, only her eyes and forehead were visible.

I'm writing to tell you that Maddy and I are getting married. We're in the process of organising the wedding, but the date will be Saturday 13th December.

Luke paused. *Do I want to invite him?* He saw Brian standing in a corner, nursing a drink and staring at everyone else dancing. Given what had happened in the past, most of the people at the wedding would not be glad to see him, himself and Maddy included. Luke wasn't even sure that Brian could be in the same room as Jemma and Raphael without a catastrophe. *He's expelled from the Keepers' Guild,* he thought. His eyes widened. *That means Maddy and I are probably out of bounds, too.*

I realise you won't be able to attend, he wrote, *but I thought I should let you know.*
Yours sincerely,
Luke

He addressed the envelope to the bookshop where Brian had last been seen, folded the sheet of paper, put it inside and sealed it before he changed his mind. 'I'll get a stamp in the morning.'

'OK,' said Maddy. 'Should I email everyone individually, or BCC them?'

'Individually,' said Luke, at once.

Maddy rolled her eyes. 'That'll take ages.'

'But a group email feels impersonal.'

'I suppose,' said Maddy. 'At least I can copy and paste the message.' She sighed, swigged some tea, and retreated behind the laptop.

'I'd better contact Ludovic,' said Luke.

Maddy's head popped up. 'Why?'

'He thinks we've gone home. It seems rude to stay on his patch and not tell him.'

'I doubt he cares,' said Maddy. 'He couldn't wait to be on his way.'

'That's a bit harsh,' Luke replied. 'The people at the John Rylands think he's a nice guy, even if they don't see much of him.'

'Maybe that's why,' said Maddy, darkly.

'I'll send a quick text,' said Luke. 'Jemma gave me his mobile number.'

Maddy shrugged. 'On your own head be it.'

Luke picked up his phone, found Jemma's text and pressed on the number. He chose the option *Send Text Message*.

Hi Ludovic, he typed. *This is Luke Varney. We met earlier at John Rylands Library.*

That was the easy bit done. He thought it over, then decided to stick to the facts. *Just a quick message to say*

125

that we will return to the library tomorrow to speak further with the staff. I hope that's OK.

He deleted the last sentence. *I'll keep you informed.*

He pressed *Send*.

Maddy laughed. 'Giulia's replied in Italian! I think she's a bit excited. Hang on while I translate it…'

'Actually, would you mind if I used the laptop? I want to transcribe my notes and create case files. You can do what you're doing on your phone.'

Maddy looked up, startled. 'Um… OK.' She turned the laptop towards him.

Luke opened Excel and created a new spreadsheet. He wasn't sure what to do with it, so he created a new document in Word and saved it as *John Rylands Library – Known Facts*. He made another document, which he headed *Interview Notes*.

His phone buzzed. Astonishingly, it was a reply from Ludovic.

Thank you for letting me know. I'm not sure what you expect to find, but good luck. L.

Luke snorted. *Not sure what you expect to find*, indeed. *I'll sort that library out*, he thought. *Just you wait.*

'I've had a reply from one of the Golden Age ladies!' Maddy exclaimed.

'Oh good,' said Luke. He opened his notebook, peered at his scrawled notes, and began to type. Every so often he paused to sip his tea and watch Maddy tap at her phone. He still felt uneasy, but much less so than he had earlier. That had to be a good thing.

CHAPTER 15

Maddy woke in the dark and sighed. It wasn't unprecedented, but it was unusual. *What time is it – two thirty? Three thirty?* She hoped she could get back to sleep.

She could hear regular breathing next to her. *You made it to bed then*, she thought. *At least you're not having another hunting dream.* While the sitting-room sofa was very comfortable, a night on it didn't appeal.

Sending save-the-date emails and putting the replies in new folders named *Wedding: Coming* and *Wedding: Not Coming* had taken some time, largely because she'd had to do the second half on her phone. Meanwhile, Luke sat opposite frowning at the laptop.

When she yawned and stretched at eleven o'clock, he looked up and said 'I'll just finish this.'

'Do you want another drink?' she asked.

'I won't be long.'

So Maddy had got ready for bed, including loosening her long dark hair so that it would spread attractively over the pillow, and waited.

And now it was morning. Hopefully.

Curiosity got the better of her and she reached for her phone, which she had left on the bedside table. Her fingers met fabric.

Of course: the curtains of the four poster. Luke must have drawn them when he came to bed.

In itself, that was perfectly reasonable. The apartment wouldn't have light-filtering film on the windows. However, she still felt slightly irritated, though she couldn't have said why.

Eventually she found the edge of the curtain and a line of light made her blink. Carefully, so as not to let it fall on Luke and wake him, she groped for her phone.

6.30. That's pretty good!

Maddy swung her legs down, eased herself through the gap in the curtains, and padded to the kitchen to make a pot of tea.

The laptop was sitting on the table. Maddy opened the lid and entered the password: it was a work laptop, and the password was known to all employees.

No documents were open.

Maddy opened the file manager. At the top were two documents: one called *Known Facts*, one called *Interview Notes*. She opened both and read.

It didn't take her long: either Luke had summarised his notes or they had been short in the first place. Not to say scanty.

Maddy fetched her notebook and transcribed what she'd written about their interview with Yvonne. It didn't seem enough. So she poured herself another cup of tea and created a new document called *Observations*.

Yvonne – middle-aged woman, calm and unflappable, inclined not to take Jess seriously. I doubt she believes in the supernatural. But she was kind to Jess and looked after her.
She let a guided tour into the reading room but limited it to five minutes and stayed throughout. Does she play by the rules?

She typed *Ludovic*, and thought some more.

Assistant Keeper for Manchester. Hard to get hold of, but came to the library specifically to speak to us yesterday. Appears middle-aged, casually dressed, bald with thick glasses. Short and stocky. Speaks with a strong Mancunian accent.

Why am I typing this? It isn't a missing persons notification. Her finger hovered over the delete key, but she left it.

Ludovic thought either that Jess imagined what happened in the reading room, or it was specific to her. He was annoyed when we discovered it wasn't, through Luke's experience. When Luke called for help, he went in and stopped it, just like that. He decided we were too junior to deal with it, and more or less told us to go home. She could feel her eyebrows drawing together. *Luke sent a*

129

message to tell him we are continuing the investigation.

Other staff: Soraya, Josh. They've seen Jess's video but only know about the incident through what they've heard from others. No direct involvement. Probably still worth interviewing.

Jess saw the event in the reading room and alerted Jemma. Very important. Yvonne says she likes fantasy and magic. Interviewing Jess is our priority today.

She saved the document and minimised it, then drank her cooling tea. Her watch said twenty past seven. *Time we were both up*, she thought. *We need to talk over what we learned yesterday before we return to the library.*

She padded to the bedroom. 'Luke?' she called.

There was no response.

She checked the window curtains let in no direct light, then drew the bed curtain. 'Luke, it's nearly half seven.'

'Ummfff.' Luke rolled on his back and began to snore.

'Oh, *really*.' Maddy climbed on the bed and patted his shoulder, with increasing firmness.

'Wassat... I'll look in the stockroom.'

'Luke!' Maddy barked.

His eyes shot open. He stared at the ceiling for a moment, then his gaze swivelled to Maddy. 'No need for that.'

'There is,' said Maddy. 'We need to discuss the case, then go for breakfast before we hit the library.'

'We're not hitting the library. We're visiting it.'

'I've typed my interview notes and made observations,' said Maddy. 'I'm going to take a shower. I made tea, but it's probably stewed. Can you make a fresh pot? I won't be long.'

When she emerged from the bathroom, wrapped in two large towels, she found Luke sitting at the laptop in his T-shirt, reading. 'What do you think?' she asked, unwrapping the towel round her head and rubbing her hair.

'Yeah, it's good,' said Luke. 'Have you left me a towel? How bright is it in the bathroom?'

'There isn't a window, remember. And yes, there are two big towels for you too.'

'Thanks.' He left the room, and a minute later she heard running water.

She checked the teapot, which still held the dregs of the tea she'd made. She tutted, emptied it, refilled the kettle and switched it on, then went to get dressed.

When Luke returned, wearing black jeans and a midnight-blue shirt, Maddy was sitting at the table in one of her bookshop outfits, drinking a fresh cup of tea. 'We need to talk about Jess,' she said. 'And what we learned yesterday.'

'You could have made me a cup,' said Luke.

'Tea's in the pot. I didn't know how long you'd be.'

'Fine.' He went into the kitchenette. 'I've read your notes, and presumably you've read mine,' he said, with his back to her. 'So we're both up to speed.'

'We haven't discussed them. Or what approach we'll take with Jess.'

'I assume I'll take the same approach as I did with

Yvonne,' said Luke. 'That went well.'

'As you took the lead on that, surely it's my turn today,' said Maddy.

'That doesn't make sense: we ought to be consistent. Anyway, you're better at taking notes. I'd miss things.'

'In that case, you should practise.'

'We're investigating a serious incident,' snapped Luke. 'Not deciding who'll make the tea.'

'Because I always make the tea,' Maddy retorted.

'So you'd rather I'd made the tea than read what you've written? I thought it was important that we get up to speed before we *hit the library*.'

She scowled. 'Why are you being like this?'

'I'm not being like anything,' said Luke, wearily. 'Jemma asked *me* to investigate what's going on at the library, and you're supporting me. That means I do the interviews and I make the decisions.'

Maddy stared at him. The worst of it was that he was right. When she had agreed to come, it had been solely to support Luke. Now she was here, everything felt different. 'OK,' she said, quietly.

It wasn't OK. But sorting things out at the library had to be their priority, not arguing over who did what. 'Let's go and find breakfast.'

***

Maddy parked Gertrude in the same space as before. As they walked down the side of the library, Luke's phone rang.

He fished it out of his pocket. 'Hi, Jemma. Yes, everything's fine, going in for more interviews... Uh-huh.

132

Oh good… Yes, I'll tell her. OK, bye.' He put the phone in his pocket. 'That was Jemma.'

'I gathered,' said Maddy.

'She says everything's fine at both bookshops. Apparently it's been fairly quiet. She said to say hi to you.'

'I'd have said hello back, if I'd known.'

'We're here now.' He strode in and Maddy followed, trying not to frown. *What am I, chopped liver?* But there was something else: something she couldn't put her finger on.

Maddy felt surprise when they asked for Jess at reception and Soraya said casually, 'Oh yeah, she's already in.' She took them to a small room opposite the stairs. 'She won't be long,' she said, and withdrew.

'Got your notebook?' asked Luke. 'Hope you sharpened your pencil.'

Maddy put her notebook and pen on the table without replying.

When she arrived, Jess had done her best to cancel out the effect of her uniform T-shirt by teaming it with a long, floaty, sari-patterned skirt, Doc Marten boots and a bright neckerchief. Her long straight hair was tomato-red, and both her arms had sleeves featuring tattoos of mermaids, vampires, elves and Celtic knots.

'I like your arms,' said Maddy, on impulse.

Jess jumped. 'Oh, thank you.' She smiled nervously and tucked her hair behind her ear, which had several piercings and a smallish black gauge in the lobe.

'Good morning, Jess,' said Luke. 'Do take a seat.'

She perched on the edge of the chair opposite them.

'I'm Luke, and this is Maddy.' She had half expected him to say *my assistant Maddy.* 'We've come from London to talk to you about what happened in the reading room.'

'I suppose you think I made it up too,' muttered Jess.

'We're just trying to get at the truth,' Luke said, soothingly. 'I'll ask you some questions, and I'd like you to answer as fully and honestly as you can.'

Jess folded her arms. 'I hope this won't take long.'

Her answers were short and to the point. She had been shelving books in the right-hand gallery. She had been there maybe five minutes before the trouble started. She had assumed the thumping was someone moving boxes, since the library was closed to the public. Then she had realised it was coming from directly beneath her. She had looked over the balcony and seen the books moving and the glass shaking. She had gone down and told them to stop, filmed a short video and run to fetch someone.

'Did you lock the door?' asked Luke.

'No,' said Jess, 'I did a runner. If you'd been there, you'd have done the same.'

'So if someone was in there, they could have left at that point.'

'How could one person have done all that?' said Jess, querulously. 'Besides, if they could make books move by magic, they could unlock a door, couldn't they? Anyway, the whole team has keys to the building.'

'Just asking,' said Luke. 'Why did you film the video? Were you planning to post it on social media?'

'No!' cried Jess. 'I'm not sure why. I think because I couldn't believe it was happening. If I filmed it and there was nothing on the video, fair enough. But there was.' Her eyes narrowed. 'What are you trying to say?'

Luke made a note and sat back. 'I'm not *trying* to say anything. I'm trying to understand what really happened.'

'I've told you what really happened.' She sat back too, bottom lip jutting out. 'Are we done?'

Maddy moved her chair forward with a sharp scrape. 'Jess, can I ask how you felt when you looked down and saw what was happening?'

Jess glanced at her, startled. 'How I felt?'

Maddy nodded. She could feel Luke gazing at her, but kept her focus on Jess.

'I felt...' Jess paused. 'When I went into the room, I felt fine. Happy, even. It had been a nice quiet day. People love to visit the library, but it's hard to do your job when you have to go round people taking selfies and blocking aisles and . . . being people, I suppose. I was meeting a friend later, for drinks and a film, so I was thinking about that. Then I heard the thumping. At first, it didn't bother me. When I realised where it was, I thought people might be running in the reading room, although it sounded more like a herd of elephants. But when I saw the books moving, I felt dread. As if it was the end of days. Books aren't meant to move. Not unless *we* move them.'

A bead of sweat trickled down Maddy's back, though the room wasn't hot. She felt Jess's dread, sensed her dry mouth and throbbing pulse. 'Did you feel anything else?'

Jess considered. 'Curious, I guess. Why were the books doing it?'

'And you'd never seen anything like that before,' said

Luke.

Jess shot him a withering look. 'Of course not. Have you?'

'Yes,' said Luke. 'More times than I care to think about.'

'Luke, I'm pursuing a line of enquiry,' snapped Maddy. She turned to Jess. 'You said that you told the books to stop. How did you feel when they didn't obey you?'

Jess shrugged. 'I never thought they would. I felt angry, and sad. I wanted to help but I couldn't do anything. I was afraid they'd break the glass and hurt themselves, and somehow it would be my fault. So I shot a video on my phone then ran for help.'

'Which door did you leave by?' asked Maddy.

'The main one: it was nearest.'

'When you left the room, did you feel as if you were being pulled back?'

'Oh no. If anything, it was like I had a strong wind behind me. I didn't think anything of it at the time, but now you've said that…'

'That's really interesting,' said Maddy. 'Did you get that, Luke?'

Luke scowled at her. 'Yes, thank you.'

'Good,' Maddy said quietly. 'Jess, I can tell that what happened has affected you. Would it help to return to the reading room with one or both of us? It may help you put it behind you.'

'No way,' said Jess. 'Even if nothing happened, I'd always be looking over my shoulder.' She lowered her voice. 'I've asked to transfer to the other John Rylands, permanently. I love working here, but books moving on their own is a step too far. If I can't transfer, I'll try to get library work somewhere else. Given that libraries are closing all the time, though, that may take a while.'

'I understand,' said Maddy. 'Thank you very much for your time.'

'No problem,' said Jess. She stood, went to the door, then paused. 'If *you* want to talk to me again,' she said, addressing Maddy, 'I don't mind.' Then she left.

'We agreed that I would lead the interview,' said Luke, once her footsteps had died away.

'We did,' said Maddy, 'but you were winding Jess up and failing to ask important questions. How someone felt may be as important as what they did.'

Luke rolled his eyes. 'You're susceptible. You tuned in to her, so naturally you think you understand her better.'

'Maybe I do.' She put her notebook in front of Luke, then took his. 'Let's make sure we got everything.'

She stared at his spidery handwriting, but took little of it in. She was intensely sorry for Jess, who might have to put up with the situation or find any job that would do.

Is my job safe? she thought, remembering the little she knew of Jemma's call. *If the Friendly Bookshop can manage without me, what will I do?* And she could answer neither question.

CHAPTER 16

Luke read Maddy's notes. Her writing was clear, rounded, the notes organised with bullet points. Even so, he didn't feel they had got anything new from the interview with Jess. 'Well, that was a washout,' he said, passing the notebook back.

Maddy raised her eyebrows. 'Really?'

'What did you get from it?'

'I got a real sense of how she must have felt,' said Maddy. 'I might talk to her again in a day or two, maybe explore that a little more.'

'I don't see how that will help with sorting out the reading room. If anything, you're stopping her from moving on.'

'I don't agree,' said Maddy, and folded her arms.

The word *tough* was on the tip of Luke's tongue when he saw her expression: closed, angry, and beneath that, hurt. *Why am I being mean to her? We don't have to agree on everything.* 'I may have put that a bit strongly,' he said, instead.

'I accept your apology,' said Maddy, staring at the opposite wall. Then she sighed and turned to him. 'We're both new to this. It's natural that we won't always agree.'

'That's exactly what I was thinking,' said Luke. He reread his own notes. 'I wonder if there's something to my theory that someone was in the reading room at the same time as Jess.'

'It's possible,' said Maddy. 'It's a big room, with plenty of places for somebody to skulk. But it seems unlikely. Why would someone do that? Perhaps more importantly, we know from our own experience that strange things only happen in the reading room when someone's alone.'

Luke smacked the table and Maddy jumped. 'Or so we think! What if someone's been hiding in there every time?'

Maddy gave him a puzzled look. 'Why? What's the point?'

'If I'm right, and we can work out who it is, maybe we'll be able to get at the motive.' Luke rubbed his hands. 'We know when the incident with Jess happened. Let's see who was in the building.' He stood and headed for reception, notebook in hand. He was vaguely aware of Maddy talking about keys, but his mind was elsewhere.

Soraya was at the reception desk, talking to a young woman with a small girl in a pushchair. 'Oh yes, everything valuable is under glass,' she said. 'You've no need to worry. The lift is more than big enough for your wheels and it goes to all floors. If you do encounter steps, there's usually a member of staff around who can help you with the pushchair.'

'Brilliant,' said the young woman. 'Come on, Aisling,

let's go.' The toddler crowed as she was pushed towards the lift.

Soraya turned to Luke. 'I take it your meeting went well,' she said. 'Jess came over a minute ago looking happier than she's been for a while.'

'Yes,' said Luke, 'we've got some interesting new information.' He leaned on the desk. 'Would it be possible to find out who was in the library when the incident happened?'

Soraya pursed her lips, thinking. 'I don't see why not,' she said. 'Give me a second: the staff rota's in a funny place on the network.' She stared at her screen, clicking her mouse. 'So you're making progress.'

Luke drew himself up. 'Yes, I am.' He heard an exasperated little huff behind him. 'We are.'

'Good, because I'm sick of having to explain to visitors that the big impressive room is closed. They come from miles away. Library nerds.' She grinned at him, then looked at her monitor and clicked a few more times. 'Got it,' she said. 'Monday is a closed to the public day, so we don't have many people in. That afternoon, the staff in were Jess, obviously, Yvonne, Josh, me – except school rang to say my daughter threw up in PE, so I left at half past one.'

'So Jess, Yvonne and Josh,' said Luke.

'Yes, and Bill.'

'Bill?'

'Yes, Bill.'

'We haven't met him yet.'

Soraya smiled. 'It's unlikely you will. Bill's a

140

conservation expert. He spends most of his time prowling in the archives and the stacks, conserving books, or consulting experts. I often don't see him from one week to the next, but he's almost always in.'

'Right. How long has Bill worked here?'

'For ever,' said Soraya. 'He's the longest-serving member of staff by some way. What he doesn't know about books isn't worth knowing.'

'Is he in today?' asked Luke, as casually as he knew how.

Soraya rolled her eyes. 'Maybe we should give you staff access, so you can check the rota yourself.'

'Sorry,' said Luke. 'I'm keen to speak to Bill.'

'Yes, but there's a queue. Give me a few minutes, would you?'

Luke stepped aside and browsed the book selection in the gift shop. He picked up a book on typography and leafed through it. Then he turned to Maddy, who was studying a book on suffragettes. 'We're finally getting somewhere,' he murmured.

'Mmm,' said Maddy.

The queue diminished slowly. After what seemed like half an hour, but was probably no more than three minutes, Soraya looked his way and beckoned. He walked over. Maddy stayed where she was.

'I've checked, and Bill was in first thing, but he left at half nine,' she said.

'Do you know if he'll be back?'

'I doubt it,' she replied. 'He's gone to Leeds for a bookbinding seminar.'

'Right. Will he be in tomorrow?'

Soraya clicked the mouse. 'There's nothing to say he won't be,' she said. 'That's the best I can do. Good luck tracking him down. He's elusive at the best of times.'

'Mmm,' said Luke. 'We'll go for a coffee and a chat. It's been a productive morning, so far. We want to keep up the momentum.' He glanced at Maddy, who was deep in the suffragette book. 'Don't we, Maddy?'

She looked up guiltily and put the book on the shelf. 'Yes, definitely. Sorry, I was miles away.'

'I was saying to Soraya that we'll go for coffee. Do you need us to sign out? We probably won't be long.'

'Please,' said Soraya, tapping the visitors' book. 'Health and safety.'

They sat in the same dark corner of the coffee shop. Luke had a large Americano, while Maddy drank tea. He took a gulp of his coffee, put his notebook and a pen on the table and got out his phone.

'What are you doing?' asked Maddy.

'I'll ring Jemma and see if she can send me a link to those social media posts about the library.' Luke frowned. 'Hopefully they're still there. From what Ludovic said the other day, I wouldn't put it past him to get them taken down.'

Maddy raised her eyebrows. 'I doubt he'd bother.' She considered. 'Then again, he might ask someone else to do it.'

Luke dialled Jemma's number. She picked up after two rings. 'Hello, is everything all right?'

'Yes, fine. Could you send me links for those Facebook

142

posts you saw about incidents in the library?'

She was silent for a good few seconds. 'I could probably find them,' she said. 'I saved the posts. But I'm on my own and there's a queue.'

'Oh, sorry.'

'So yes, but not immediately. If I find them, I'll email.'

'Thanks, Jemma. How are—'

But she had already ended the call.

'Sounds busy over there,' Luke told Maddy. 'I might need a long coffee break.' He grinned.

'Or we could interview the rest of the staff,' said Maddy. 'There are plenty of other things we can be doing. We could maybe even see if someone will take us to the reading room.'

Luke stared at her. 'Why would you want to do that?'

'To experience it. Maybe, now I've been in the room twice, it's getting used to me.'

'I imagine the reading room was pretty used to Jess,' said Luke. 'That didn't stop it from frightening the life out of her.' He drained his cup and set it down, harder than he intended. 'I'm getting another. You?'

Maddy shook her head. As he got up, she took out her own notebook and began to leaf through it.

Luke was halfway through his second cup of coffee when his phone buzzed. An email alert, from Jemma. He snatched up the phone and unlocked it. 'Here we go!'

Jemma had sent two links. *There may be other posts,* she had written, *but these are the ones I found. Good luck.*

He clicked on the first: it was dated September 24th.

I was in the John Rylands Library in Manchester

yesterday when something really strange happened.

'September 24th!' he exclaimed. 'Write that down, Maddy.'

He scanned the rest of the post.

A friend and I had had lunch at Comptoir Libanais and as I was nearby, I decided to pop into the library then get the tram home. As usual, time ran away with me and I was on the way to the reading room when a member of staff told me it was fifteen minutes to closing. I told her I'd be quick and hurried in. A couple was just leaving, and I had it to myself.

'Late afternoon,' said Luke. 'Fifteen minutes till closing time. Make a note, Maddy.'

He went back to his email and clicked the second link. Again, the incident had happened in the last half hour before closing and the person had been alone. Luke gave the day and time to Maddy, finished his coffee and stood. 'Time to go and check the rota.'

'I wonder why it's always in the late afternoon,' said Maddy. 'Because your incident was in the morning.'

'It'll depend on whether Bill's in,' said Luke. 'I'm guessing a lot of staff have left by then to pick up their kids, so he can roam free.'

'You're making him sound like the Hunchback of Notre Dame,' said Maddy. 'He's probably a slightly introverted guy who's into his work. Not unlike us.'

'We'll see,' said Luke. He strode towards the library. Maddy wasn't far behind, but he was too impatient to wait.

Soraya heaved a sigh as he approached. 'Let me guess,' she said.

'You're absolutely right,' said Luke. He turned. 'Maddy, the notebook.'

Maddy handed him her notebook with a mulish expression on her face. He riffled through it until he found the right page, put it in front of Soraya and stabbed the dates and times. 'Then, and then. Who was in?'

'Please,' added Maddy. 'If you don't mind.'

The skin on the back of Luke's neck prickled. Who was she, his mother? Not that he remembered much about his mother: that had been so long ago. He tried to think of something to say to Soraya, but she was already absorbed in the mysteries of her monitor.

'Right,' she said. 'On the afternoon of the first date, staff in were Steph and Iqbal from the other John Rylands, Bill, Olivia the placement student, and Jess. On the second date, Olivia again, Josh, Yvonne, Steph and Bill. That was Olivia's last day with us.'

'So we can count her out,' said Luke. 'Has Steph been in this week?'

'She isn't usually here,' said Soraya. 'I was off with labyrinthitis for quite a while, so she came in to cover me.'

'So the common factor is Bill.' He leaned forward. 'I'm sorry to ask again, but was Bill in yesterday morning?'

Soraya clicked away, looking resigned. 'He was,' she said.

'That's all I need,' said Luke. 'We'll be in the room by the lift, if that's OK.'

Soraya's expression conveyed that they could go anywhere they liked, so long as they stopped bothering her.

As soon as the door had closed, Luke punched the air.

145

'Yes! Got him!'

'I really don't think you have,' said Maddy. 'You don't know that he had anything to do with it. You haven't even met the man.'

'Exactly! He's hiding.'

'He's doing his job.'

'You're just annoyed that you didn't spot it,' said Luke. 'All that stuff about feelings, when what we needed was evidence.' He sat down, took out his notebook, cracked his knuckles and began to record his breakthrough.

Maddy sat opposite him. 'You found a correlation,' she said. 'It may not mean anything.'

'I know what I think,' said Luke, and continued writing. He considered telling Maddy that sour grapes didn't taste very nice, but decided to be the bigger person.

CHAPTER 17

Maddy stared at Luke, who was writing in his notebook with a smug little smile on his face, as if he hadn't just dismissed her theories on the case. Or possibly because he had.

'I beg your pardon?' she said.

Luke looked up. 'I'm not saying you're wrong, exactly.'

'Yes you are. You're saying that feelings don't matter and all that does are facts, as you call them. You're grasping at the first two things that go together and making a finished case of them.'

'I'm building a case, yes,' said Luke. 'Obviously we can't do anything until we've met this Bill. So I'm thinking of the best questions to get the truth out of him.'

'What about interviewing the rest of the staff?' asked Maddy. 'What about actually talking to the people who posted on Facebook? Or is the time of day when they had their experience the only thing that matters?'

'All in good time,' said Luke, and carried on writing.

'Shall I get on with that while you set your trap?'

Luke put his pen down. 'There's no need for that. And I can't say I like your tone. I'm not the Witchfinder General.'

Maddy felt anger bubble up. Normally she'd take deep breaths, make an excuse to go somewhere else and calm herself. Today was not that day. In fact, she welcomed the heat rising inside her. 'You know who you remind me of?'

Luke opened his mouth but she didn't wait for him to respond.

'Lennox Nash, that's who. Swanning around as if you're the boss of everything. Well, you're not. And you're not the boss of me. I'm taking a break.'

'We just had a break,' said Luke.

'And I'm taking another. It isn't as if you need me, is it? Except to ferry you about in Gertrude.' For a moment she thought of getting in the camper van and heading to London, leaving Luke high and dry in Manchester.

'Maddy! What's got into you?'

His reproachful tone cut her to the quick. 'Right, that's it. That is *it*.' She wrenched the door open, slammed it behind her and stormed off, only stopping to sign herself out at the desk.

'Unbelievable,' she muttered as she crossed the road, eager to put as much distance between herself and Luke as possible. She saw a narrow side street, took it and found herself weaving through a grid of tall buildings, studded with boutique shops, coffee bars, pubs and the occasional little green square. *Hopefully this'll make it less easy to follow me.*

He won't bother, she thought. Then: *More fool him. Let him sit and work on his stupid theory.*

What if he's right?

Maddy slowed her pace. *Maybe he is.* She shrugged. *That doesn't mean he should dismiss my ideas.*

She turned onto a main road. Now she'd stopped rushing, she had more time to take the city in properly. There was a church, which paradoxically looked much less like a church than the library did. She thought about going in but decided she might be disappointed. The idea of cool and quiet was attractive, but she wanted to be among people.

That was odd: normally the reverse was true. After a busy day in the bookshop, even though she enjoyed chatting to the customers, Maddy generally longed to go home, lock the door, and spend the evening either in solitude, or with Luke.

Who had betrayed her. That was how it felt.

I never expected to get caught up in the case. Now I have, he won't listen. He's only interested in his own ideas and theories. He doesn't care what I think.

Until recently, she had never thought of Luke as ambitious. When he had proposed to her, she had assumed they would carry on more or less as they always had, working as assistants in two linked bookshops, and the sole change would be living together.

As you always had, said a mocking little voice in her head. *You've been going out for – what – a year?*

A year is a long time, thought Maddy, but despondency crept over her like a lowering dark cloud. *Have I been wrong about him all along?*

'Mind out, love,' said a man's voice.

'Oh, I'm so sorry,' said Maddy, but he held up a hand in acknowledgement and carried on.

Then she realised she had no idea where she was or where she was going. Did it matter? That was what phones were for. And it was a welcome luxury not to have to be in a specific place at a specific time. Her breaks in the bookshop usually fitted around Jemma's meetings, or when Luke would be free for lunch. *Why do I have to fit around him?* she thought, with growing resentment.

She stepped into a little alcove and gazed about her. The smart, shiny shops had given place to less polished establishments and the people looked bohemian. *Good. This feels more my sort of area.*

Two people passed, talking and laughing. Both were very pale, with black clothes and jet-black hair. *I wonder where they're off to*, she thought, and before she knew it she was following at a respectful distance.

A few minutes later, they went up the steps of a building called Afflecks. She had no idea what it sold, as the windows were covered, but it called itself an emporium.

Well, she thought, and followed.

Inside was an Aladdin's cave of quirky little shops. A vintage clothes shop, a jeweller, a seller of crystals, a record shop…

Maddy wandered, browsed and climbed to the next floor, taking everything in. She considered a jet necklace, she breathed in the smell of sandalwood, she flicked through racks of loud shirts that Luke wouldn't have been seen dead in.

Then she fell in love.

In a large, dark clothes shop, she spotted a mannequin half in shadow, dressed in a long black dress. As she got closer, she saw that the dress had a black lace overlay, most visible in the trailing sleeves and the short train puddling on the floor.

My dress!

She had waited to buy a dress for the wedding, partly because she wasn't sure what she wanted, and partly because she didn't want to tempt fate by doing it before Luke had his documents. But now...

You didn't want to be in the same room as him half an hour ago, said the mocking little voice. *Now you're looking at a wedding dress.*

If I buy it, thought Maddy, *it'll be for me. Anyway, I don't even know if it fits yet.*

Ten minutes later, she was admiring herself in the narrow, speckled mirror of a changing room composed entirely of nylon curtains. *It's as if this was made for me. I can't leave it behind, I just can't.*

She came out of the changing room and gave the shop assistant a twirl, partly to judge his reaction and partly to have an excuse to stay in the dress a little while longer.

'Wow!' he said. 'You're the Queen of the Night!'

'Thank you very much,' said Maddy, suddenly dignified.

At last, back in her normal clothes, she braced herself and found the price tag. *Is that all? For this?* She took it to the counter and paid before anyone could say there was a mistake.

'Enjoy,' said the assistant, as he folded the dress tenderly and placed it in a large paper bag.

'I shall,' said Maddy.

As she left the shop, she realised she was hungry. She had breakfasted lightly, as usual, and arguing and walking had clearly burned a lot of energy. She walked until she came to a nice-looking deli and ordered a hummus and falafel wrap and a glass of cloudy lemonade. How decadent to eat in such a wholesome place, among people on their lunch breaks and others in workout gear, knowing she had the dress of her dreams under the table.

Imagine wearing that in the library.

Maddy pushed the thought away and took another bite of her wrap, but as she chewed she visualised herself in the cloister, posing at a window, standing by the curved balustrade outside the door of the reading room—

Don't be silly.

She longed to see it – no, to experience it. To be the Queen of the Night in her own Gothic palace. *I can tell people it's for an art project. Maybe someone will even take photos for me.* Luke never crossed her mind.

He did when she re-entered the library, though. 'Oh, you're back,' said Josh. 'Didn't think we'd see you again today.'

Maddy's eyes narrowed. 'How come?' she asked. 'You weren't on the desk when I left.'

He grinned. 'Luke said you'd gone off in a huff when he signed out.'

'Did he,' said Maddy. 'Is he still out?'

'Yup,' said Josh. 'He left maybe twenty minutes ago.

152

He said he was going to do some thinking.'

'More like a long lunch,' said Maddy.

'I did wonder,' Josh replied, and they shared a conspiratorial grin. For a moment Maddy felt mean, then decided that what was sauce for the goose was sauce for the gander.

'Has Luke interviewed any more staff besides Jess?' she asked.

'Not as far as I'm aware,' said Josh. 'I swapped places with Soraya five minutes after you left, and he was in the back room.'

'OK,' said Maddy. 'I might get on with that in a bit. I'll take a wander first.'

She wandered downstairs to the disappointingly modern toilets, got changed in a cubicle then appraised herself by the washbasins. Her Birkenstocks were not what she would choose to go with such a dress, but they were almost invisible. She undid her plait and let her hair tumble over her shoulders. Even in the harsh light of the bathroom the effect was impressive. She put her clothes and other belongings in the paper bag, got in the lift and headed for the cloister-like corridor on the first floor.

She was rather disappointed by people's lack of interest. There were a few curious glances, but generally everyone went about their business, discussing where to go for lunch, how the trams were running, or why there wasn't a café in the library. Maddy leaned against the window and took a selfie, but when she checked it a man in a baseball cap had strayed into the shot at the last moment and was looking straight at the camera with a puzzled expression.

She tutted and took another, but the moment was lost.

She went up the stone steps to the landing outside the reading room, but a young woman had parked her pushchair there and was sitting on the floor, giving her baby a bottle. A party of teenagers were taking up a small ledge, showing each other their phones, giggling and eating snacks.

Where can I find peace and quiet in this place? Maddy thought, crossly. A sign was in front of the door: *READING ROOM CLOSED TODAY.*

Maddy edged towards it. No one noticed.

She tried the door. To her astonishment, it opened. She checked no one was looking, slipped in, and closed the door.

Strangely, as soon as she was alone, she felt calm. That in itself wasn't strange: she liked to be alone. But the day before she had refused to stay in the reading room with Luke, and now she was here by herself. *See how far you've come.*

She took a tentative step forward, then another. She eyed the statue of Enriqueta Rylands, but nothing happened. Just to be sure, she walked quickly until she had passed the first display case. That seemed to be the limit of the safe zone.

Maddy strolled to the other end of the room, venturing into the alcoves, running her hand along the desks, inspecting the books, which were as motionless and well behaved as if there had never been a disturbance in the library. She peeped at a little spiral staircase enclosed in a stone recess. It was roped off, but who was there to stop her? Then the reality of negotiating the steep, narrow steps in a full-length gown and train brought her to her senses and she moved on.

She tried the door to the periodical room, but it was locked. *You're supposed to be taking photos*, she thought. She propped her phone on a radiator cover, set the timer, and took a few steps backwards until she was leaning against a pillar.

A brief flash of light.

Oops. She hurried to the phone. When she picked it up, though, there she was, pale in her black gown, her hands touching the pillar as if she was somehow bound to it and her hair cascading down.

'Wow,' she breathed.

She turned the flash off, then took a photo of herself by a bookcase, half in shadow, and another with a background of carved wood. As she went to get her phone, she heard a slight noise above. *Time to go.*

She had left her bag by the door. She hurried past the display cases—

Her foot slipped.

Oh no.

Maddy turned and her foot slid on the parquet. She kicked off her shoes and grabbed the nearest display case.

The sense of being towed eased and she exhaled. *That was too close for comfort*, she thought. *I'll see if the door at the other end is open.* She edged along the display case, continuing to grip the side.

Then Maddy found she was going backwards even as she tried to move forwards, and screamed. She managed to put out her hands to block whatever horror was about to happen. They touched white marble. For a moment, she felt as if her hands had actually sunk into the statue, but when she looked, they were resting on the folds of Enriqueta Rylands' dress. And the feeling eased.

'Sorry,' muttered Maddy. She grabbed her bag and seized the door handle, half expecting it to be locked, but it opened easily and she stumbled out, slamming the door.

'Can't you read?' said a voice she knew.

Panting and dishevelled, Maddy met the disapproving eyes of Yvonne.

CHAPTER 18

Yvonne's expression changed from annoyed to concerned as she gazed at Maddy. 'Oh no. That room's given you a scare, hasn't it? Come up with me and I'll make you a brew.'

'I – I'm fine,' gasped Maddy.

'You aren't: you're as white as a sheet. That notice is there for a reason,' Yvonne said mildly.

'I'm sorry. I was… I was just—'

'Never mind that. Do you want to lean on me? We'll take the lift.' And like a caring but bossy sheepdog, Yvonne shepherded Maddy upstairs, sat her down, and made her drink a cup of very sweet tea, gently shushing her whenever she tried to talk. 'Shall I ring your colleague to come and get you?'

Maddy shook her head. 'I'll message him.' She reached into her bag and the sight of her trailing sleeve reminded her of what she was wearing. 'I have to get changed first. Is there a bathroom up here?'

Yvonne looked puzzled. 'Why do you need to change?'

'He can't see this dress.'

'I can see it, so... Oh, you mean— I didn't know you two were, um, together.' Then she looked puzzled all over again. 'A black wedding dress?'

'We have a theme,' said Maddy.

'Oh. Right. Go and change, then, and I expect you back in ten minutes or I'll come and find you.'

Maddy escaped to the basement toilets, which were mercifully empty. She allowed herself a lingering glance in the mirror. Yes, she was pale, but not significantly more than usual. She sighed, went in the cubicle and got changed, folding the dress with care. 'I don't blame you,' she whispered to it as she placed it reverently in the paper bag.

As Maddy put on her trousers and stripy top, her face burned. *What made me do it?* The thought of what Luke would say didn't help.

When she was dressed, she sat in the cubicle for a while, wondering what to tell him. Then she realised that if she didn't get a move on, Yvonne would no doubt break down the cubicle door. She pulled her hair into a ponytail – no time to plait it – and hurried to Reader Services.

'That's better,' said Yvonne. 'You can't beat hot sweet tea for a reviver, can you?'

Maddy nodded. 'Can I stay for a bit?' The thought of going downstairs, where she might see the people who had watched her pose in the dress, made her skin itch.

'Of course you can,' said Yvonne. 'No one's in, for a miracle. Now, get on and phone lover boy.' She grinned. 'Now you've got colour in your cheeks.'

Maddy took out her phone and opened her messaging app. *I'm fine but I had a small experience in the reading room*, she typed. *I'm in Reader Services with Yvonne x*

Her thumb hovered over the delete button, but she left the X there and sent the message. She tried not to dwell on their last exchange. Would Luke come? Would he even reply? He might be having lunch, or have switched off his phone.

A tick appeared next to the message, followed by three dots. *On the way x*

A wave of relief swept over Maddy. *After I was so horrible to him. I said he was like Lennox Nash. I don't deserve him.* She blinked hard.

'You're in shock,' said Yvonne. 'I'll get the kettle on.' She retrieved a biscuit tin from her drawer. 'Have one of these while you're waiting.'

Five minutes later, Maddy heard a sharp rap and saw Luke's face at the window.

'Your knight in shining armour's turned up,' said Yvonne, rising unhurriedly and going to the door. 'She's in here, safe and sound,' she said.

Luke dashed past her and swept Maddy into his arms. 'Are you all right? Did that thing hurt you?'

'I'm fine,' said Maddy. 'Although you're squashing me.'

He slackened his hold and looked into her eyes. 'Are you sure? What happened?'

'I went into the reading room—'

'Why?'

'I just did.'

'How did you get in? Did someone let you in?'

'The door wasn't locked.'

Yvonne sighed. 'I left it for two minutes to fetch something, assuming that people would respect the notice. And of course I got waylaid.'

Luke released Maddy and sat in a nearby chair. 'What happened?' he repeated.

'It was fine until I went to leave. The statue pulled me towards her.'

'The Enriqueta Rylands statue?'

'Yes. For a moment I thought my fingers were sinking into the stone, but when I looked, they weren't. Then the pull stopped and I got my things.'

Luke frowned. 'The pull stopped?'

'Yes. I said sorry and left and Yvonne was outside.'

'I was coming back anyway and I heard the scream, so naturally I got a wiggle on,' Yvonne put in.

'I screamed when I found myself going backwards,' said Maddy. 'That was the worst bit.'

'When did this happen?' Luke took out his notebook.

'Twenty minutes ago. Maybe twenty-five.'

Luke turned to a new page and wrote *New Incident*, followed by the date and time. Then he closed the book. 'What would you like to do? Shall we head to the Airbnb? Then you can rest.'

'Good idea.'

Luke took her hand and helped her to her feet. 'Can you drive, or shall we get a cab?'

'Cab,' said Yvonne.

'I can drive,' said Maddy. 'I'm fine now, and Gertrude's . . . a sort of automatic.'

160

Yvonne looked sceptical. 'Make sure you rest. Maybe we'll see you tomorrow, if you're fit.'

'I'm fine,' said Maddy. 'It was just a – a surprise.'

'A nasty surprise,' said Yvonne, firmly. 'Go on, off you go. And make sure you hide that dress.' She clapped a hand to her mouth. 'Oops.'

'What dress?' said Luke, once they had left. 'Why would you hide it? What's going on?'

'What's going on is that Yvonne couldn't keep a secret if you glued her mouth shut,' said Maddy. 'I went to a shop and bought a dress, and it's the one.'

'The one?' Comprehension dawned. 'Oh, the one!'

'Exactly. That's why Yvonne said I should hide it.'

'She's seen it? Why did you show her?'

Maddy sighed. 'I'll tell you when we get to the Airbnb.'

'Are you sure you're safe to drive? What if we're in an accident? Not that I'm saying you'd cause an accident, not at all, but…'

Maddy imagined Gertrude wrapped around a lamp post, Luke slumped unconscious in his seat, with a gash in his forehead, and a stern police officer telling her to wind down her window while sirens blared. 'Maybe we should wait,' she said. 'Let's go in the back room, if it's free.'

They took the lift downstairs. Maddy waited outside the room while Luke had a word with Josh. He returned and they went in.

Luke moved his chair so that they were sitting close together. 'I asked Josh not to disturb us,' he said.

'Thanks.' Maddy twisted her hands together in her lap. 'I'm sorry about . . . what I said earlier.'

Luke gave her a rueful smile. 'I'm sorry for behaving in a way that made you say it. Once you'd gone and it was too late, I realised I was getting too big for my boots. I need you, Maddy. I love you. I hate it when we fight.'

'So do I,' Maddy murmured.

'Anyway, your experience has exploded my theory about Bill. He's in Leeds today. I doubt anyone could control the behaviour of a library from across the Pennines.'

Maddy let out a giggle.

'Do you need anything?' asked Luke. 'A glass of water? More tea?'

'Not more tea,' said Maddy, with a grimace. 'If someone lost a leg, Yvonne would give them a big mug of hot sweet tea and leave it at that.' She glanced at the water cooler in the corner.

Luke took the hint and fetched two cups. They drank for a while in silence. 'Would you mind if I asked some questions?' asked Luke. 'While it's fresh in your mind.' He put a hand on her arm. 'If it's too much, just say. I can get us a cab. Gertrude will be fine here for the night.'

'It wasn't that bad,' said Maddy. He was looking at her expectantly. 'Go on, get your notebook out.'

Luke took out his notebook and a pen, and found the page he had started earlier. 'OK. Can you tell me, in your own words, exactly what happened while you were in the reading room?'

Maddy felt her face grow hot again. 'I need to tell you something first,' she said. 'I was wearing the dress.'

Luke stared at her. 'Why?'

'I was coming back from Afflecks, where I bought it, and I suddenly thought how well it would suit the library. It's long and black and it has a train, and the library would be the perfect setting. So I came here, put it on in the toilets, then went to take selfies.'

Luke's pen stopped. 'You never take selfies. You hate selfies.'

'I know, but I looked so good in the dress. So I went to the cloister – that long corridor by the exhibition rooms – but there were tourists everywhere and I couldn't get a decent shot. People kept photobombing me. So I went to the curved balcony outside the reading room, but that was busy too. The reading room was right there, and when I tried the door it opened. So I went in and I got some really good photos. I'd show you, but…'

'You're wearing the dress,' said Luke.

'I heard a noise from the gallery and decided to head off before anyone saw me and asked what I was doing. As soon as I was past the last display case, I felt a pull. The rest you know.'

'So the statue, or whatever it was, let you go when you said sorry?'

'No, it let me go first. Then I said sorry. It seemed a bit rude, clutching the statue's dress. So I got my bag and left and Yvonne was right there.'

'OK,' said Luke, as he wrote. 'So Yvonne left the room open and she was on the landing when you came out.' He frowned. 'I wonder if she was in the gallery, too.'

'You can't possibly think Yvonne is behind this,' said Maddy. 'I know there's a theory about the most unlikely

163

person, but I'd say it's impossible that it's Yvonne.'

Luke huffed quietly. 'I agree. It's just annoying, because that would be a neat solution. Even though she hasn't been around for the other incidents.' His face lit up. 'Unless two people are working together.'

'Let's concentrate on facts,' said Maddy. The corner of her mouth turned up a fraction. 'Rather than feelings.'

'Oh, stop it,' said Luke, and gave her a squeeze. 'I'm already embarrassed enough.'

'Me too,' said Maddy. 'Let's forget about it and get on with solving this case and going back to London.' As she said it, she felt a pang. 'I shall miss the library.'

'Will you? We've only been here two days.'

'It's such a wonderful building. That's why I wanted the photos.'

'I still think that's weird,' said Luke. 'Why would the library want to scare you?'

'It isn't the library,' said Maddy. She thought for a while. 'Yvonne means well, but whenever there's an incident in the reading room she acts as if the person it happened to has had a horrible experience and must be really scared. I *was* scared, when I couldn't control my movements, but I felt something else, too. I'm trying to work out what it was, but with Yvonne and now you acting as if a nightmare has happened, it's hard to put my finger on it. When we spoke to Jess, she wasn't entirely scared by it, either. There's something deeper, or at least different, that we need to get to.'

'Right,' said Luke, looking sceptical. 'That won't happen today. Let's get out of here. Maybe once you've

164

had a rest it will become clearer.'

At the reception desk, a man in a tweed jacket and corduroy trousers was talking to Josh. He was perhaps in his fifties or early sixties, with a sandy beard and wire-rimmed glasses. Josh replied, then the man made for the door.

'See you tomorrow, Bill,' called Josh, and Bill raised a hand as he walked off.

Maddy and Luke exchanged glances and ran after him.

CHAPTER 19

'Bill! Wait!'

Bill was walking quickly and purposefully across the pavement. He didn't react to his name being called.

Luke put on a burst of speed and touched Bill's arm. Bill jumped, half-turned and stepped away. 'Excuse me?' he said, seeming both affronted and apprehensive.

'I'm sorry,' said Luke, as Maddy caught him up. 'We were calling you, but you didn't hear.'

'Oh. I'm slightly hard of hearing,' said Bill. 'Especially with traffic noise and so on.' He gestured to the slow-moving cars. Then he frowned slightly. 'I don't think we've met.'

'Luke Varney.' Luke held out his hand. After a second, Bill shook it. 'This is my colleague, Maddy Shenton. We're investigating the recent incidents at John Rylands Library. That's why we want to speak to you.'

Bill's frown deepened. 'Investigating? You don't look like police. What incidents?'

'The things that have been happening in the reading

room,' said Luke, patiently.

'Oh, that.' Bill considered. 'I thought that was rather minor.'

'It seems that not everyone agrees with you,' said Luke.

'It would be a dull world if everyone agreed with each other, wouldn't it?' said Bill.

Luke felt his inner temperature rise. 'Aren't you supposed to be in Leeds?' he said.

'I was, yes,' said Bill. 'When I got to the station, my train had been cancelled. I was cutting it fine anyway, and even if I'd taken the next train, I would have missed the presentation that I wanted to hear. So I decided to return to the library.' His eyes narrowed slightly. If anything, the wire-rimmed spectacles made his gaze more intense, not less. 'Why so curious?'

Luke met Bill's eyes, with an effort. 'We're talking to all staff as part of the investigation. As you're here…' He kept his tone as light and casual as he could. Beneath it, though, he felt tense. He didn't like the vibes radiating from Bill. And he didn't want to give anything away.

Bill looked at his watch. 'I've got time for a quick chat over coffee. It *will* be a quick chat, as I have very little to say on the matter.' He headed for a cafe across the road and Luke and Maddy followed. Maddy raised her eyebrows at Luke, who shrugged in reply.

Bill ordered an espresso for himself and asked what they wanted. 'Just water for me, thank you,' said Maddy.

'I'll make it another espresso,' said Luke. Somehow, it seemed important to match Bill. *This isn't a competition*, he told himself. *You're being silly*. But Bill was definitely rubbing him up the wrong way. Especially now that his theory was back in the game.

Bill took his espresso and headed for a small table. 'So where are you both from?' he asked.

'We're from London,' said Luke. 'We're Associate Keepers.'

'Oh,' said Bill. 'Associate Keepers, eh.' His eyes twinkled behind his spectacles. 'That's new.'

'So you know about the Keepers' Guild,' said Luke.

'I do,' said Bill. 'I'll save you time by telling you that I have never seen or felt anything I would consider odd in the library.'

'How long have you worked there?' asked Maddy.

Bill crossed his legs and inspected the side of his shoe. 'Many, many years. Probably since before you two were born.'

'I doubt it,' said Luke.

Bill looked him up and down with an expression that suggested Luke might be something unsavoury. 'Indeed,' he said. 'Who have you spoken to so far at the library?'

'Well, Jess, obviously.'

'And?'

'We've spoken to Yvonne.'

Bill sipped his espresso. 'And?'

'We met with Ludovic.'

The espresso cup clacked into the saucer. 'Ludovic's graced us with a visit, has he? What a shame I missed him.'

'I take it you're not a fan,' said Luke.

Bill gave him a haughty look. 'I am not a fan, as you

168

put it, of anything,' he said coldly. 'I *appreciate* people and things. I *value* their skills and attributes. I appreciate and value some people and things more than others.'

'So you don't like him.'

'As Ludovic is an infrequent visitor to the library, I haven't seen enough of him to decide.' Bill finished his espresso. 'We're quite capable of managing ourselves and the institution, without having occasional drop-ins from someone who can barely manage to pass the time of day.'

Interesting, thought Luke. *Wounded pride? Resentment that Ludovic is senior to him? Anger that they're responsible to a central organisation?*

'Who else have you spoken to at the library?' asked Bill.

For a moment Luke considered lying, but he had a feeling that if he did, Bill would check up on him. 'That's it so far, apart from you,' he said. 'We arrived yesterday.'

'If you were prepared to chase me down the street,' said Bill, 'that suggests you're very keen to speak to me. Is there a reason for that?'

Luke could sense Maddy fidgeting beside him. *Do I tell him what we know?* He met Bill's eyes and felt as if he had no choice. If he lied, Bill would see right through it. 'There is the point that, according to staff records, you are the only person who has been in the library on every occasion when an incident has happened in the reading room.'

Bill considered this, his face expressionless. 'Am I? That's an interesting statistic. Although you would do well not to confuse coincidence with causation. I advise you to be careful in how you proceed.'

'Do you,' said Luke.

'Yes, I do. And I have nothing more to say on the matter.' He stood up. 'Good day to you.' And with that he walked out of the café.

Luke turned to Maddy. 'Did you hear that?'

'I did,' said Maddy.

'He practically fled the interview, and as good as gave me a warning.' Luke snorted. 'Him and whose army.'

Maddy put her hand on his arm. 'Careful, Luke. If he *is* behind the incidents in the library, he's clearly powerful.' She looked thoughtful. 'What was it he said? That he'd never seen or felt anything in the library that he'd consider odd.'

'Exactly,' said Luke. 'I have a distinct feeling that what he considers odd and what other people do are two very different things. From the sound of it, he's been allowed to do as he likes. Though it doesn't explain why all this has started happening.'

Maddy's eyebrows drew together and she drank some water. 'Unless it's something to do with...'

'With what?' said Luke. 'Come on, Maddy, spit it out.'

'Didn't Yvonne or someone say that the director of the library went on sabbatical a few weeks ago? So at the moment the library is directly under Ludovic.'

'Ohhh. That makes a lot of sense.' Luke gazed at Maddy. 'So what do you think? Is Bill doing this stuff to be a thorn in Ludovic's side?'

'It's possible,' said Maddy. 'Though it seems childish.'

'You heard him,' said Luke. 'He clearly can't stand

Ludovic. Maybe he's trying to make the point that Ludovic's not the boss of the library. Even if that means putting the library's flagship room out of use.' He huffed. 'Talk about cutting off your nose to spite your face.'

'That's terrible,' said Maddy. 'That poor building, getting caught in a stupid spat between two people who ought to know better.' She turned to Luke. 'What are you going to do?'

What can I do? was Luke's first thought. *I can't stand up to Bill, and I don't want to drag Jemma or Raphael here to do it. This is my case.* He glanced at Maddy. *Our case.* 'We should meet with Ludovic again. I'll send him a message.' He pulled out his phone.

'I agree,' said Maddy. 'What will you say?'

'Nothing but the truth,' said Luke, tapping away. 'Hang on a minute, and I'll show you.' He finished his message and put the phone in front of Maddy.

Hi Ludovic, hope you're well. We've discovered that Bill is the only staff member who's been in the library every time an incident has happened. We've just spoken to him. He said he had nothing to say about the incident and tried to warn us off. Could we meet with you to discuss? Thanks, Luke and Maddy

'That covers it,' said Maddy. 'Send it, and see what he says.'

Luke pressed the green button and the phone whooshed. 'Now we wait.'

They didn't have to wait long. Maddy was halfway

171

through her glass of water when Luke's phone buzzed.

'Here we go.' He picked it up and unlocked it. 'It sounds as if you've got your man,' he read, from the screen. 'Please keep that to yourselves. I'll call at the library first thing tomorrow and we can discuss what to do. Good work.' He closed the message and put the phone down. 'Boom.'

'Well done,' said Maddy. She drank some water, gazing at the facade of the library opposite. 'That's it, then. We'll fill Ludovic in tomorrow, and he'll sort Bill out while we head home.' She sighed out a breath. 'I'll miss this place. I like what I've seen of Manchester.'

'So do I,' said Luke. 'We can always come and visit.'

'Maybe we could stop in on our way to Whitby,' said Maddy. 'For our honeymoon.'

'Maybe we could.' He took her hand and squeezed it. *We've done it. OK, I did most of the thinking, but Maddy helped.*

'I suppose we'll go back to being bookshop assistants,' said Maddy. She sounded rather sad.

'Hopefully we'll get to do more of this,' said Luke. 'Now we've solved one case.'

I hope so, he thought. *For now, I wouldn't mind a break to sell books, eat cinnamon rolls and marry Maddy. That would suit me down to the ground.*

CHAPTER 20

'Do you think we'll leave today?' asked Maddy, as Luke carried the suitcase to the door.

'It's possible,' said Luke. 'Depending on how this meeting goes. I figure we may as well be prepared. If we're needed, we can always ask Jemma for another day. We have the code to the key safe, so we can return later.'

'I guess.' Maddy gazed around the flat. 'I'll go and check we haven't left anything in the bedroom.'

She walked through and stopped by the bed, stroking one of the four-poster's curtains. She had spent time the night before vacuuming and going round with a duster, and cleaned the kitchen worktops that morning. It still didn't feel like time to leave, though. 'Hopefully we'll come back,' she whispered into the soft folds.

Luke walked into the bedroom. 'I'm sure we will,' he said. 'But this investigation is more or less over. All we have to do is make sure Ludovic knows the facts.' He encircled her in his arms.

Maddy looked up at him. 'I have a feeling this isn't

finished,' she said.

Luke grinned. 'You really have fallen for that building, haven't you?'

She shrugged. 'Maybe I have. I must admit, it's been a great trip. I never thought I'd enjoy it as much as I have. Even with the weird things that have happened.'

'Those are pretty standard, in our line of work,' said Luke.

'For you, maybe,' said Maddy. 'But yes, we can go home and I can carry on with the wedding planning. Especially now I have a dress.'

'Which I still haven't seen.' Maddy had done all the packing for exactly that reason.

She beamed at him. 'You will. When the time is right.'

He kissed her forehead. 'Can't wait. Going home is part of that.' He frowned slightly. 'To be honest, I'll be glad to hand the case over and wash my hands of it.'

'Haven't you enjoyed it?'

'Mostly, but it wasn't what I thought it would be.'

'In what way? We've interviewed people, we've discussed the case, we've visited the location, we've checked documentation.'

'I suppose I expected more magic. And more books.' The frown was still there. 'I wasn't going to say, but I had an odd dream last night.'

'What, a hunting dream? You didn't – I didn't see any of the usual signs.'

'No, it wasn't like a normal hunting dream. I didn't taste blood. We were both there, chasing someone round the library. I assume it was Bill, but we never saw the

174

person clearly. It was as if we were in a maze, but we never caught them or found the centre. We just kept going down corridors and through rooms and staircases and... I felt exhausted when I woke.'

'You poor thing.' Maddy looked at her watch. 'We've got time before the library opens. Why don't we go somewhere nice for breakfast and you can have red meat.'

'I'll be fine,' said Luke. 'I've already had my drink for today.'

'Have you?' That was decidedly odd. Luke normally left his daily drink of vegan blood substitute until lunchtime or later, as an additional boost. 'It must have been quite a dream.'

'It was, rather. Come on, let's put our stuff in Gertrude and leave the key. Depending on how the meeting goes, we could be on our way by eleven o'clock, or even earlier.'

The traffic, as ever, was merciful and Gertrude's special parking space was waiting. Maddy reversed in, wondering why she'd ever been nervous about driving the camper van. The difficulty would be driving anything else after getting used to Gertrude's little ways.

They walked down the narrow road towards Deansgate and the library entrance. 'I wonder what *first thing* means to Ludovic,' said Luke, in an attempt to lighten the mood. 'I hope we don't have to wait long.'

As it turned out, they didn't. They were barely through the door when Ludovic bounced over. 'Glad you could make it,' he said. 'Get yourselves signed in and I'll give you an update.'

'An update?' said Luke.

'Yup.' He folded his arms and waited while they wrote their names in the visitors' book. 'Lovely. In we go.'

He headed for the lift and pushed the button for the second floor.

'We're going to the reading room?' said Maddy.

'Why not?' said Ludovic. 'It's quiet and private, since the public aren't in yet.' He leaned in slightly. 'Fact of the matter is, I thought you should be the first to know, seeing as you uncovered the key detail. I don't want any other staff listening in.'

'Oh,' said Maddy. She felt disorientated, but couldn't be sure whether that was the impact of the news or the motion of the lift.

When they arrived in the anteroom, Ludovic produced a large keyring from his pocket and jingled it. 'Keys to the kingdom.' He looked rather smug. He unlocked the door and motioned them in. Maddy thought he might lock the door behind them, but he merely closed it.

He led the way to the centre of the room, among the study tables. 'Here's what happened. When I got your message yesterday I had a think and decided a chat with Bill was in order. I arrived early doors and asked if Bill was in, and he was, so I went to his office and asked for a word. He tried all the busy busy stuff, but I wasn't having it. So I said that you'd told me about him being on the premises every time something funny happens, and asked him for an explanation. Which he refused to give. So I fired him.'

'You *fired* him?' said Maddy.

'I did,' said Ludovic. 'What else am I supposed to do?

Give him a warning? Suspend him on full pay? What he's been doing is gross misconduct, in anyone's book. Frankly, it's a health and safety nightmare. I've given him an hour to clear his desk and say his goodbyes, then that's it. End of story.'

'I . . . I thought we were having a discussion this morning,' Luke faltered.

Ludovic waved a dismissive hand. 'We could, but what's the point? You've already told me the important bit: anything else is detail. I'm too busy to pussyfoot around playing Mr Nice when the reputation of the library's at risk. Get it done and move on, that's my motto.'

He checked his watch. 'Well, unless you have anything to add, I guess it's time for thank you and goodbye. I'll email your boss and tell her you did a great job.' He headed for the door. After a moment, Luke followed.

Maddy stayed where she was and took a moment to look round the room. *I'll miss you*, she thought, and reached out to stroke the table beside her. As she touched it, the wood buckled beneath her fingers. 'What the—'

Luke stumbled as the floor bulged. 'What the heck?' he cried.

'Something's happening,' said Maddy. She coughed as stale, musty air hit the back of her throat.

Luke ran to her. 'Come on, Maddy, we need to go!' He gave her a gentle pull and she took a halting step forward, watching the floor in case it misbehaved. All around them, the books banged on the glass, which rattled threateningly.

What if they break out and come for us? thought Maddy. She wanted to scream, but her throat felt so tight

177

that she could barely draw breath.

'I am up to *here* with this,' said Ludovic. 'I told Bill, no funny business. I should have walked him off the premises myself.' He gazed at the heaving balconies, the contorting stained-glass windows, the melting display cases. 'What a palaver. Right.' He walked into the middle of the room and stood, feet planted firmly apart, rolling with the floor.

He raised his arms. 'Enough!' he cried.

Streams of silver sparks shot from his fingers and struck the centre of the ceiling, then ran down the pillars like mercury. The strange liquid ran over the balconies, the bookshelves, the tables, the display cases, but like mercury, it left not a trace. As it passed over each part of the reading room, every stone and piece of furniture returned to normal.

'That's better,' said Ludovic, as the mercury sped across the parquet floor and the red carpet in the aisles. 'Don't worry, it'll go round you two.'

The silver fluid sped round their feet and gathered itself until it was a sphere no bigger than a ping-pong ball lying at Ludovic's feet. He picked it up, squeezed it, and showed them an empty palm.

'That was amazing!' said Luke. 'How did you even do that?'

'Experience,' said Ludovic, and winked at him from behind his black-framed glasses. 'Right, now that's over, you two can be on your way. It's a long drive to London.' He grinned. 'I'm sure you know the way out.'

Luke made for the door, gazing around him as if he couldn't believe what had just happened.

178

'I-I want to say goodbye. To this room,' said Maddy. Her mind was in a whirl.

She walked slowly towards the door at the other end of the room, running her hand along the display cases as if to check that each one was back in its normal shape. Her stomach was churning, her heart hammering. *I'm not sure I can drive. Not after this. Gertrude may be doing the work, but...*

She paused and took a deep breath to calm herself. But the air, while not as close and musty as it had been, was not as fresh as usual.

You're probably imagining things, she thought, and carried on walking, quickening her pace a little. Then a little more, but that wasn't a choice she had made. Something was pulling her.

She looked up and saw the statue of Enriqueta Rylands. 'It's happening again!' she cried.

'Honestly,' said Ludovic, and she felt herself being pulled back until she was beside him. 'You all right?' His right arm was raised to eye level, and he was making a pinching motion with his thumb and forefinger.

'Yes, I'm fine,' said Maddy.

Luke ran to her side. 'I'm sorry, I didn't realise till you shouted.'

'It's best that you two go,' said Ludovic, with a serious expression. 'I'll lock this room, find Bill, wherever he is, and escort him off the premises myself. Then I'll call a staff meeting and break the news, to make sure he can never return.' He twisted his hand, still making the pinching motion, escorted them to the anteroom and locked the reading-room door. 'I'm going on a Bill hunt.' He rubbed his hands. 'Safe journey back to London. Hopefully, if I see you again, it'll be under nicer circumstances.' He gave them a nod and strode off, head bobbing.

'That was impressive,' said Luke, turning to Maddy. 'I'd love to know how he did that.' Then his expression changed from curiosity to concern. 'Maddy, are you all right? Maddy!'

Maddy swallowed. 'I'm... No, I'm not all right.' She put her hand to her forehead, which felt clammy, and found she was shaking. 'Something's wrong,' she whispered. 'Really wrong.' Her legs gave way and she sank onto the floor.

CHAPTER 21

'Come on, Maddy, we can't stay here.'

Luke tried to lift Maddy, but she was a dead weight in his arms. He stood up. *What am I going to do?* he thought. *What if someone comes and sees her like this?* He felt his face flush.

Then he thought: *What must she be feeling?*

He sat down and put an arm round her. 'Maddy,' he whispered, 'what's wrong? Can you tell me?'

'I don't know!' she wailed. 'But it's terrible.'

Luke managed to suppress a sigh. 'Maddy, it's over. What we saw was something Bill did. Ludovic will get rid of him and everything will be back the way it was. This is a reaction to what you experienced a few minutes ago.'

Maddy looked up, her face streaked with tears. 'So why don't you feel it too? Or do you?' She frowned. 'Are you hiding it?'

'No, of course not.'

Why don't I feel the same? he thought. Then he remembered how easy it had been for people to manipulate

Maddy in the past. 'Maddy, it's because you're susceptible. Or sensitive, if you prefer. Obviously what's happened is that Bill has influenced you somehow. He probably did with Jess and those other people, too.'

'Why?'

'I have no idea,' said Luke. 'But this isn't doing you any good. The case is closed. Bill was behind it – he's as good as admitted it – and Ludovic's got it all in hand. To be honest, I don't like the idea of you being anywhere that Bill can get to you. The best thing for us to do is go back to London. There, we're out of his reach, and closer to Jemma and Raphael, who can protect you.'

Maddy looked woebegone. 'I can't drive in this state,' she quavered.

Luke sighed. 'I don't expect you to, Maddy.' *Quite frankly, I wouldn't want to be on the road with you at the moment.* 'What you can do is rest in Gertrude for a while. She'll keep out any bad vibes.' He gazed at the book-lined walls, the woodcarvings executed with such skill and care. 'I don't know what it is about this library, but it's – it's bad for you.'

'Don't say that,' said Maddy, as if he had insulted her. 'I love this place.'

'Maybe,' said Luke, 'but it doesn't love you. Otherwise, why would it treat you this way?'

Maddy looked accusingly at him. 'You said that was Bill.'

'Does it matter? The point is that our work here is done. We're needed in London, so we have to leave.' He stood and held out his hands. After a few seconds, Maddy

182

wiped her eyes and took them.

He pulled her to her feet. 'That's better.' He gave her a quick hug, then put an arm round her waist and helped her to the lift. *A few more minutes*, he thought, *and we can wash our hands of this place for good.*

Soraya's eyes widened as Luke supported Maddy through the foyer. 'What happened? Is she all right?'

'She had a bit of a funny turn,' said Luke.

'No I didn't,' said Maddy. 'It's the building. It's trying to tell me something.'

'She'll be fine when she's had a rest,' said Luke, firmly, as he signed them both out. 'It's been lovely to meet you and the team, Soraya. Thank you for your help.'

Soraya frowned. 'What, you're leaving?'

Ludovic hasn't had a chance to tell them yet, thought Luke. 'Yes,' he said. 'Our part in the investigation is done. You'll hear more in due course, I'm sure.'

'Oh. All right. Well, it was nice meeting you too.' She held out her hand and Luke shook it briefly.

'We'd best be off,' he said. 'Long drive to London.'

'Yes, take care,' said Soraya, but she looked vaguely troubled.

'Maybe you're right,' said Maddy, as they walked slowly down the narrow road at the side of the library. 'I do feel a bit better.'

Luke fought the urge to say *I told you so*. 'There,' he said. 'You'll feel much better once you're safe in Gertrude. Have you got the keys?'

Maddy fished in her bag and handed the keys over.

When they reached Gertrude, Luke opened the back

door and helped Maddy in, then climbed in after her and closed the door. He patted one of the benches. 'It isn't exactly a four poster,' he said, with a smile, 'but hopefully it'll do.'

'Thanks,' said Maddy. She lay down on the bench and Luke found a coat to cover her with. She still looked pale, and her eyes seemed haunted. 'You will stay with me, won't you? I— I don't want to be alone.'

'Of course I'll stay with you,' said Luke. He crouched beside her, took her hand and stroked her hair.

Maddy sighed and closed her eyes. Before long, her breathing slowed and her hand grew limp.

Luke stood, his thigh muscles protesting a little, and climbed through to the driver's seat. He leaned back to ease the key from his trouser pocket and fitted it in the ignition. *Should I?* he thought.

Driving off had been in his mind almost since he'd suggested Maddy rest in Gertrude. It would be so easy, now she was asleep, to begin the journey home.

But it's illegal. For one thing, I don't have a licence. And I don't know how to drive.

Gertrude would take care of the driving. She probably wouldn't let anyone stop us, either.

If Maddy was awake, she'd never let me do it.

Maddy needs to get away from this library, whether she wants to or not. I can help her do that.

Luke made sure the volume on the radio was fully down, then turned the key until there was a soft click.

Various lights illuminated the dashboard, including one he hadn't seen before. It was next to the petrol gauge. It

184

was red. And the needle was stuck at empty.

It's probably nothing, he thought. *When I start her up, the needle will go to halfway.*

He pressed the left pedal, like Maddy did, and turned the key again.

Gertrude gave a polite little cough and was silent. The petrol gauge stayed exactly where it was.

Luke huffed. *Great. We're stuck.* He scowled. *Thanks for checking the petrol, Maddy. Off in your own world, as usual.* He knew it was unfair even as he thought it, but venting his bitterness made him feel slightly better.

He looked round at Maddy, who was sleeping peacefully. *Maybe this is another of Bill's tricks. Unless it's some sort of thing between the library and Maddy. Why does it want to keep her here?*

Luke sat back in his seat. Then he texted Jemma.

Would it be possible, hypothetically speaking, for someone to bond with a building?

His thumb hovered over the *Send* button. He added *Just curious* and sent it.

He stared through the windscreen at the narrow road and the buildings ahead until a reply came perhaps a minute later.

Yes, definitely. Look at Folio and Burns Books. He was definitely bonded with the bookshop till Luna came along. And the kittens, obviously.

Another message followed perhaps half a minute later. *Any reason for asking?*

Luke replied: *As I said, just curious.*

The next response was quicker. *All OK there?*

185

Luke stared at the message, wondering what to type in response. *My fiancée might be in an unhealthy relationship with a library* wasn't the sort of thing you could tell your boss. Not even one as understanding as Jemma.

We've solved the case, he typed, then deleted it.

Sort of. We're working through some things. We're both fine, more or less. He pressed *Send.*

Tell me if you need help x

Thanks, he replied, and put the phone on the passenger seat.

Gertrude never runs out of petrol, he thought. *It doesn't make sense that Bill would want us to stay. Not when I was the person who shopped him to Ludovic. Plus I'm pretty sure that Gertrude is impenetrable to all but the strongest magic, given who her owner is.*

So if someone isn't controlling Gertrude, running out of petrol must be her decision. She wants us to stay.

And if she wants us to stay, there must be something else we have to do.

He considered phoning Jemma, telling her everything and asking for advice, but swiftly rejected the idea. *This is supposed to be my case. Well, mine and Maddy's, now.*

What would Jemma do? Or Raphael?

He closed his eyes and searched his memory, but what came up wasn't a picture of Jemma or Raphael, though both were present.

It was Hermione Dawes, soothing a distressed book and wrapping it in her scarf. She hadn't grabbed it, she hadn't shouted at it. She had treated it with care and respect.

He recalled Ludovic shouting at the reading room to

186

pack it in. Shooting silver missiles at the ceiling and forcing the room to behave. The rest of the library staff, instead of trying to work out what was wrong in the reading room, had locked it and refused to go near. A different kind of punishment, but a punishment nonetheless.

That's it, he thought. *We need to be kind to the building. Maybe then we'll discover that something else is the matter. Something deeper.*

Carefully, he climbed through to the back of the van and sat on the other bench, watching Maddy. She was still pale – not that she was pink-cheeked at the best of times – but the shadows under her eyes weren't as dark and her breathing was regular.

I must tell Maddy what I've realised. He stretched out a hand, then paused.

She needs all the rest she can get. Because if I'm right, and we have to return to the library and try a new approach, it won't be me leading it. It'll be Maddy.

CHAPTER 22

Maddy took a deep breath, then pushed open the door of the reading room. The slight creak made everyone within turn and stare, but for once, she didn't mind. For once, she felt pretty.

She lifted her lacy black skirts a fraction to make walking easier, and moved past the statue of Enriqueta Rylands, who seemed to be looking down on her with approval. The display cases had been moved to the sides, creating a red-carpeted centre aisle. She wasn't sure that having their guests sitting on the display cases was good library etiquette, but no one had said they couldn't. Behind her walked a procession of cats. Folio and Luna strolled side by side, tails up, followed by the kittens, who for once were behaving themselves.

She could see Luke peeping around their guests, and Raphael standing in front of the statue of John Rylands. There was no music, but the silence, punctuated by the occasional gasp as she passed each display case, was better.

At last she came to a stop beside Luke. He was dressed in black and midnight blue, with a velvety dark-purple rose in his buttonhole, and in her opinion, he had never looked handsomer. Next to him stood Jemma.

Luke put his hand on her shoulder and patted it. Then he shook it.

'What's wrong?' she said, but the words didn't come out right. She blinked once, twice—

And there was Luke, wearing a bottle-green shirt and crouching beside her. *Why am I lying down?* she thought, and struggled to sit up. *You can't lie down at your wedding. That isn't right.*

'Maddy... *Maddy...*'

Her surroundings came into focus, but for a moment she couldn't place where she was.

'We're in Gertrude, in Manchester,' said Luke. 'Were you dreaming?'

'Yes.' Maddy rubbed her eyes, hoping it might make the library return, but no. 'I was so happy,' she murmured. 'We were in the library, getting married.'

'I'm sorry I woke you,' said Luke. 'It's just... If we're staying on in Manchester, we must tell Jemma.'

'Wha... Stay?'

'Yes,' said Luke.

'I thought... You said it wasn't safe, and we'd done everything.'

'I've been thinking,' said Luke. 'While you were asleep. And I realised something. We need to be nice to the library, and you're in charge of that.'

'Me? In charge?' Maddy folded her arms, staring at

189

him. 'I don't know what I'm doing. Why have you changed your mind?'

Luke shrugged, then looked sheepish. 'When you were asleep, I thought about starting Gertrude up and leaving. Driving home.'

Maddy's eyes widened. 'You can't drive. You don't have a licence.'

'I'm not proud of it. It was an impulse, because you were so upset. Anyway, Gertrude says we're out of petrol. She won't let us leave. So I got to thinking, and… I texted Jemma. I reckon you've bonded with the library, and that's why you feel stuff that I don't.'

'Right.' Maddy attempted to take this in.

'And I was thinking about Hermione Dawes. When she did the assessment, she was nice to the book and she got the best results. She respected it. We need to respect the library. That's what Ludovic hasn't been doing. He's been forcing the library to behave and it's making the building cross.'

'Do we have any water?' Maddy's mouth was dry, and she wasn't sure it was just thirst. Everything seemed to be rushing at her far too quickly to take in.

Luke passed her a water bottle. The liquid moistened her throat, but her heart was still beating too fast.

'So you and Jemma texted about me while I was asleep.' It was a statement, not a question.

'No,' said Luke. 'I asked her whether it was possible for a person to bond with a building, and she said yes it was, because Folio bonded with Burns Books.'

'I'm not a cat,' said Maddy. 'If I am bonded with the

library, what does that actually mean? Does it mean I can't leave?'

'It can't do, can it? You're here.'

'Here being ten feet from the library,' said Maddy. 'Don't tell me I have to spend the rest of my life in Manchester. I mean, it's nice, but it isn't exactly what I had in mind. What about our wedding? Would we have to get married in the library? And our honeymoon, and—'

'I'm sure it isn't that,' said Luke, taking her hand in his. It reminded her of the dream, and she relaxed slightly. 'I mean, Folio is happy in either shop now.'

'For the last time, I'm not a cat!' said Maddy. 'This could be serious. What if I can't go back to work? And what about you?' She swallowed to try and keep her rising panic in. 'I don't know what I'm supposed to be doing. What am I leading? How? I can't do it on my own.'

'You don't have to,' said Luke. 'You've got me.'

'Yes, but...' She paused, thinking of a way to say what she needed to without being rude. 'It's our first assignment,' she said, eventually. 'Be honest: neither of us knows what we're doing. We don't have years of experience and strong magic, like Jemma and Raphael do. If we mess this up, that's it. We won't get to do this again.'

'I don't want to go running to Jemma,' said Luke. 'That would be nearly as bad as messing this up. If we can't be trusted to get on with things and use our initiative, what's the point in being an Associate Keeper?' He looked at her, his brow furrowed and his expression pleading.

'I know how much this means to you,' said Maddy. 'It's important to me, too. I do see your point. But...' She

191

gazed around her, marshalling her thoughts, and her eyes fell on a medium-sized cardboard box stowed under the bench. 'The books!' she said, and pointed. 'Let's open the box.'

Luke's frown deepened, which was unexpected. 'It may not be the right time yet,' he said. 'What if we open it and nothing's any use? Or something worse happens and we've used our chance?'

'I don't think the bookshop works like that,' said Maddy. 'Maybe the books will be able to change if we need to look again. Anyway, your argument means we'd never look inside the box. What's the point of that?'

Luke sighed. 'I hope you're right.' He managed a half-smile. 'You're the boss.' He pulled the box out and put it on the bench. 'It's really light.'

The box was sealed with packing tape. Maddy picked at it with her fingernail. 'Shall I open it, or do you want to?'

Luke considered. 'Let's take an end each.'

A few seconds later, the tape was off. The flaps of the box had lifted slightly, as if to beckon them in.

'Here goes,' said Maddy. She opened both sets of flaps, put her hand in and drew out a chunky paperback with a bright cover. 'A Literary Guide to Manchester,' she read. 'The authors are Selwyn Teasdale and Ludovic Wright.'

'Is that our Ludovic?' asked Luke.

'There can't be that many people called Ludovic in a position to write this book.'

She turned to the back of the book. There was a photo of Selwyn Teasdale, an unexpectedly young man in a blue open-necked shirt. Beneath was a photo of Ludovic

Wright. Maddy studied it, then passed the book to Luke.

'That's obviously him,' said Luke. 'Why is it in the box? Unless Ludovic knows something about the library that he hasn't told us yet.'

Maddy took back the book and read the biography next to the photo.

Ludovic Wright was born in Manchester and has never wanted to go anywhere else. After finishing university, he joined the library service, rising to the position of head archivist of Manchester Libraries...

She examined the photo again. Ludovic stood there, arms folded, dressed as usual in a black T-shirt and jeans and wearing his trademark round black-framed spectacles. But in the photograph he wore a warm, friendly smile. He looked like someone you would chat to about your weekend, someone who would share memes on reading and libraries, someone who would suggest a group night out and possibly take you who knew where in the name of fun, but in a good way. 'He looks like Ludovic . . . but he also doesn't.'

Luke gave a little huff, then peered over her shoulder. 'I see what you mean, but that's probably his photo smile. It's not his fault that he's got the male equivalent of resting bitch face.'

Maddy put the book on the bench and reached into the box. She had to scrabble about. At last her fingers found soft leather and she drew out a small, slim hardback, maroon with gold tooling, decorated with a pattern of intertwining stems and leaves. It appeared venerable, though not particularly ancient. There was no title, just the

193

initials BJF. The same initials were on the spine. 'What's this?' she said, and opened it.

In contrast to the elaborate cover, the title page was plain. *Being an updated version of Ephemera From A Life Of Transformation. Incorporating New Discoveries on Metamorphosis.* She closed the book and handed it to Luke. 'You look at it. I don't want to.'

'I'm not sure I do,' Luke replied. 'I remember how weak Raphael became after he shape-shifted.' He peered at the book. 'This seems familiar, but I can't think why.'

Maddy sat forward, her elbows resting on her knees and her chin cupped in her hands. 'Ludovic, but not Ludovic,' she said. 'Could that be possible?'

'Of course it's possible,' said Luke. 'I saw Raphael shift from a random tourist into Drusilla, and I never suspected. And we both saw him do it in Berkshire.'

'It's just so weird,' said Maddy. She shivered. 'I can't believe I'm even thinking it. If the man we met isn't Ludovic, who is he?'

'Time for another book,' said Luke. 'Go on, Maddy.'

Maddy took a couple of deep breaths, then reached into the box. 'There's one book left,' she said. 'No wonder it was light.' Her fingers closed on another leather-bound book. She drew it out and peered in. 'That's it.'

'Well, go on,' said Luke. 'What is it?'

This book was bound in green leather. Its title, in gilt capitals, was simply *ACCOUNTS*.

'Accounts?' said Maddy. 'Who publishes accounts? Whose accounts?' She tutted, and opened the book.

The title page was different: *Adventures of a Young*

Buck on the Grand Tour. No author was listed. The date of publication was 1840.

'What on earth…?' said Maddy.

'Did someone mix up the binding?' asked Luke.

'Maybe…' Maddy opened the book at random and started at the left-hand page.

…and I found myself drinking a rough Sangiovese wine with the brigands who had attempted to kidnap me. We got on famously, and I indicated that I would be interested in experiencing a day – or rather a night – in their life.

So the men outfitted me as one of their own, in black boots, breeches, a serviceable jacket and a villainous cap. I added an eyepatch to render myself less recognisable, and they armed me with a pistol and a cutlass.

We sallied forth, and I may say that I have rarely spent a more exhilarating night. We stopped carriages and relieved women of their jewels and men of their money and pocket watches. We took their horses and rode them until they foamed at the mouth, then broke into a great house and stole from the wine cellar while the inhabitants cowered upstairs. Then we rode into the night, drunk with wine and our own daring.

I marvelled at myself. Who knew I could be a robber, an adventurer, a man who could take whatever I wanted? I truly believe that night shaped my character in ways that have stayed with me ever since.

She closed the book. 'Whoever wrote this sounds horrible. Without knowing who that is…'

'What's the book called again?' Luke pulled out his phone.

'*Adventures of a Young Buck on the Grand Tour.*'

'I bet that isn't in Wikipedia,' said Luke, his thumbs flying over the screen.

He scrolled down the search results. 'Here we go. This is from a website about forgotten books. "*Adventures of a Young Buck on the Grand Tour* was a bestseller in its day. Its salacious content and lack of morals scandalised the newspapers, who condemned it. However, once its publisher produced a plain-covered version of the book, it became a sensation. There were five printings in 1840 alone."' He looked at Maddy. 'A marketing triumph.'

Maddy made a face.

'"The identity of the author has never been confirmed,"' Luke continued. '"However, there are three main candidates for the authorship of this book. They all took the Grand Tour and followed the described route in 1838-9, according to their correspondence. In addition, each had published a book previously with stylistic similarities. The three men were Joseph Wade, William Alder, and—"' He gasped.

'What is it?' asked Maddy, putting a hand on his arm.

'Lennox Nash senior,' said Luke. 'That's the third name. As we know, there's no senior or junior: there's only one. Thank heavens.'

'He can't be involved in this,' said Maddy. 'He's in prison.' She swallowed. 'He must be.'

Luke closed his browser and opened the messaging app. 'I'll text Jemma. She'll know. And if not, she can find out.'

Ten seconds later, his phone whooshed. 'I've said we're staying another day as well. At least.'

'OK.' Maddy's heart was banging in her chest. She leaned against Luke and together they stared at the phone, waiting.

CHAPTER 23

Luke and Maddy both jumped as his phone buzzed. Luke's thumb trembled slightly as he unlocked it. He stared at the message.

Lennox Nash is on remand at HMP Garsforth, awaiting trial. I don't know the detail, but the trial is so complex that both sides are still working on their case. I'm not even sure whether a date has been set.

He passed the phone to Maddy. 'So I guess it isn't him.'

She read the message, chewing her lip. The phone buzzed again and she nearly dropped it. 'Jemma wants to know why we're asking,' she said.

He took the phone back and hit *Reply. The box of books you gave us included one which may be by Lennox. We wondered if he could be involved.*

After a couple of seconds, three dots started to bounce under the message. It arrived half a minute later.

I don't see how that's possible and I'm not sure how I

can find out more on Lennox's whereabouts. I could ask Sergeant Hawkins.

Yes please, Luke typed. *We might be on to something big.*

The dots began bouncing immediately.

Please be really, really careful. I know you want to do this by yourselves, but I can't risk the pair of you being injured. Just say the word and we'll send help. Somehow.

A pause, then another buzz. *I'll ring Mike Hawkins now.*

Luke sighed and put down the phone. 'Jemma's ringing Sergeant Hawkins. So she isn't sure, even though she says it's impossible.'

Maddy reached for the water bottle and drank, thoughtfully. 'What do you think?' she asked, turning to Luke.

'Lennox Nash is in prison, so it's impossible that he's involved. But somehow this feels as if his mucky paws are all over it.' He visualised Ludovic: the casual outfits, the slang, the Mancunian accent. 'I'm not sure how he could bear to make himself into Ludovic, to be honest. No natty suits, no fancy language—'

'Which makes Ludovic the ideal hiding place,' said Maddy.

Luke smacked the bench with his palm. 'You're right. The way Ludovic's been floating around, attending a meeting here, a meeting there... It makes him impossible to pin down. Like Lennox was.' He grabbed the phone and scrolled through his message thread with Ludovic. 'Read these.'

199

Maddy obliged. 'What am I looking for?' she asked, after a moment.

'You know how Ludovic speaks. He calls a spade a shovel. His messages are quite formal, though, written more in the way that Lennox would communicate.' He shuddered. 'I try not to think about Lennox: I hate the idea that he's living rent-free in my head. But he's sliding his way in.'

Maddy's eyes widened as she reread the messages. 'I can't believe we didn't notice.'

'That I didn't notice, you mean,' said Luke. His brows knitted. 'Where's Ludovic's book?'

Maddy took it from under the other two books and passed it over.

Luke checked the table of contents, then paged through the book. 'Here's a chapter by him.' He read aloud. '*Let me tell you about Manchester Central Library. It's a fantastic structure, plonked in the middle of Manchester city centre as if it's come by time machine.*' He closed the book. 'There you go. That couldn't be more different from the messages.'

'This isn't looking good, is it?' muttered Maddy.

'Depends on your point of view,' said Luke. 'On one hand, Lennox is powerful, charming and scary. On the other, at least we know what we're dealing with. He's been beaten before, and recently.'

'Not by us.' Maddy twisted her hands in her lap.

'We were part of the team,' said Luke.

'Yes, but not in a defeating-people way. In a supporting capacity.' Maddy gripped the seat of the bench with both hands. 'Do you seriously think that if the pair of us met with Lennox Nash, we'd come out on top?'

Luke was silent.

'Exactly,' said Maddy. She folded her arms and stared into space. 'The best we can hope for is that we're wrong about Lennox's involvement. Maybe it's one of the other suspected authors of that book. Maybe we should research them instead.'

'Maybe,' said Luke. He felt as if Maddy had poured a bowl of cold water over him. He closed his eyes and sighed out a breath. Then he picked up *Adventures of a Young Buck on the Grand Tour* and opened it to the first page.

It is a truth universally acknowledged, he read, *that a studious young man from a promising family should spend a year discovering all the tempting pleasures he can before going to university.* His lip curled. He wasn't a fan of Jane Austen, having read the books when they first came out, but he recognised shameless and facetious pilfering when he saw it.

Just the sort of thing Lennox would say, he thought, then closed the book and put it down. He didn't have the stomach for more.

Instead, he picked up the little maroon book and opened it at random.

An important thing to remember is that to be truly undetectable, you must immerse yourself in the character of the persona you inhabit, however repellent to you that may be.

That made him smirk. *If Lennox has shifted into Ludovic, I hope he's hating every minute of it.*

He turned to another page.

You are likely to find that metamorphosis is tiring as well as tiresome. It is best to restrict yourself to short displays of your new character. Otherwise you risk becoming so fatigued that your own personality and appearance will begin to leach out, leading at best to confusion and at worst, detection.

In addition, you may find that elements of the being you have impersonated remain even after you have resumed your own identity. For example, a prominent facial feature or mannerism. Therefore it is best to seclude yourself for some time following a feat of transformation, preferably in a place with a looking glass.

I shall speak more on this topic in the chapter 'Transformation and Criminality.'

Luke slammed the book shut. His cheeks burned, his heart thumped and he was racked with guilt. 'This book,' he muttered. 'It ought to be burned. I don't know why the shop even has it. It's immoral. It's encouraging people to get away with crime.'

'But it's here for a reason,' said Maddy, taking it gently from him. 'Whether we like it or not.' She glanced at the cover and froze, staring at it as if it were a cobra about to strike.

'What is it, Maddy?'

'The initials… I can't believe we didn't see it. Don't

you recognise them?'

'Nothing springs to mind.'

'What was the Friendly Bookshop called before it became the Friendly Bookshop?'

'Oh! Of course – BJF Antiquarian Books.'

'Yes. Those are Brian's initials.'

All of a sudden, the blood in Luke's veins seemed to turn to icy water. 'How can Brian be involved? He's lost his powers and he's banned from the Keepers' Guild.'

'That didn't stop Drusilla, did it? She made a bargain with someone. Maybe Brian's done the same.'

Luke spread his hands. 'Surely he's out of the equation.'

'It could be a coincidence,' said Maddy. 'But if the bookshop is pointing at Lennox and Brian, we need to investigate that.'

'Fine,' said Luke. He stood and paced, despite having to stoop.

'Has Brian answered your letter?' asked Maddy.

'That's no good,' said Luke, still pacing. 'I addressed it from Burns Books, so any reply will go there. Given the state of the post, he may not have received it yet. It feels as if we've been working on this for ages, but it's only been a few days.'

'True,' said Maddy. She thought for a moment. 'Do you have a phone number for him?'

'I just have the address of the bookshop he works at,' said Luke. 'But I could look on the web for their number.'

He picked up his mobile and began searching. A minute later, it was ringing.

'Good morning, Curious Books and Antiquities, Hayley

203

speaking.'

'Hello, could I speak to Brian, please?'

'Brian?' Hayley repeated, as if she had never heard such a name.

'Yes, Brian. He works in the shop.'

'Oh, the old guy! I'm his replacement. He retired, you see.'

Luke sat down abruptly. 'When did that happen?'

'Umm . . . let me look in the calendar. I started on the first of September, and we overlapped by a week so that Brian could show me the ropes. So he finished on the fifth, which is . . . six weeks ago.'

'Do you know where he went?' Luke's heart felt tight, as if someone was squeezing it.

Hayley laughed. 'That's the funny thing. He was so old and doddery that I assumed he'd go into supported living or move in with a younger relative, but he said he was going travelling and he'd send us a postcard. He hasn't, though. He didn't even leave a phone number.'

Luke stood rigid, his ear to the phone. *Brian is missing, and Lennox may be too…*

'Hello? Are you still there?'

'Thanks for your help,' Luke muttered, and ended the call. 'He's left,' he told Maddy.

She buried her head in her hands. 'Oh no,' she murmured. 'If he gets hold of me again…'

'I won't let that happen,' said Luke, and put an arm round her.

Maddy looked up, wild-eyed. 'How can you stop him?' she wailed. 'Or Lennox?'

'He's been gone for six weeks,' said Luke. 'That's...' He scrabbled for his notebook and riffled through the pages. 'That's when the director of the library went on sabbatical.' He dropped the notebook and seized his phone. 'I'm ringing Jemma. This is getting worse and worse.'

The phone rang: the display said *Jemma*. He could barely control his hands enough to answer it. 'Yes?'

'Absolutely unbelievable,' snapped Jemma. He had never heard her so angry. 'Sergeant Hawkins just rang. He had to go all the way up the hierarchy of the prison and back down before he got what he needed.'

'What has he found?' Luke could scarcely breathe.

'You won't be surprised to learn that Lennox has been conducting a charm offensive with the prison staff.'

Offensive is about right, thought Luke.

'What I didn't expect was that somehow he'd manage to convince the warden on his corridor to let him out for extra fresh air. One day, presumably, he didn't return. Multiple staff were sure they'd seen him that day, but when they looked in his cell, where he should have been, he wasn't there. The last definite report of him is from six weeks ago.' She huffed. 'Who knows how many prison staff he's put under a spell?'

'Brian's missing too,' said Luke. 'Retired six weeks ago, with no forwarding address.'

'He's on the loose, isn't he,' muttered Maddy, her fists clenched. 'The pair of them, together.'

'I don't believe this,' said Jemma. 'How did you find out?'

'Too long to explain,' said Luke. 'I have to go.'

'Be careful, you two, and sit tight. I'll work something out. I don't know how, but I—'

But Luke was already helping Maddy down from Gertrude. He retrieved the keys from Gertrude's ignition, slammed and locked the door, and they pelted along the alley towards the library.

And as they ran, an image seemed burned on the inside of Luke's eyelids. Gertrude's fuel gauge, back at half mast.

CHAPTER 24

Maddy turned onto Deansgate and ran past the front of the library. She couldn't work out which emotion was uppermost. She was scared, yes, and definitely worried, but at the same time she was happy.

She slowed for a moment and ran her hand along the ancient stone wall. A thrill went through her. *I'm coming back to you.*

'Come on!' Luke called.

Reluctantly, Maddy ran after Luke. They paused outside the door to catch their breath, then went in.

'Um, hello?' said Soraya. 'Have you left something behind?'

'Not exactly,' said Luke. 'Is Ludovic still here?'

'Oh no, he's long gone,' said Soraya. 'He left before you did.'

'Right. Did he call a staff meeting?'

'Ludovic? He's not that kind of guy. He came bouncing out in his usual way and said he had to get to his next meeting.' She thought for a moment. 'I think he said

Stockport, but I could be wrong.'

'Was anyone with him?' asked Maddy.

'Well, no,' said Soraya. 'He came on his own and he left on his own.'

'So you didn't see him with Bill.'

'What is this, twenty questions?'

'Sorry,' said Maddy. 'We are asking for a good reason.'

Soraya grinned. 'It's unlikely you'd ever see Ludovic with Bill. They can't stand each other. No idea why.'

'Have you seen Bill today?' asked Luke.

'Yes, first thing this morning.' Soraya regarded them with narrowed eyes. 'Is this leading to something, or do you have time to kill?'

'Soraya, this is huge,' said Luke. 'We know the truth. We know—'

'What we know is that everything we thought we knew is wrong,' said Maddy. 'Isn't that right, Luke?'

'Er, yes,' said Luke, looking slightly hurt.

'Luke's right, too. We believe we've worked out the problem with the reading room.'

Luke's eyebrows shot up. *Have we?* he mouthed.

'OK,' said Soraya. 'What is it, then?'

'I'm pretty sure we're right,' said Maddy, 'and I'm hoping we can fix it ourselves. What we really need is backup and a witness. Could you call Jess and Yvonne and ask them to meet us at the main doors of the reading room?'

Soraya's eyebrows shot up. 'Good luck with that,' she said. 'If you can get Jess in the reading room, I reckon you can do anything.'

Five minutes later, Luke, Maddy and Yvonne were waiting on the curved landing outside the reading room. The *READING ROOM CLOSED TODAY* sign was still in place. Yvonne had a biscuit tin under her arm.

'I don't think she's coming, Maddy,' said Luke.

'She has to,' said Maddy. 'We need her. It has to be Jess.'

'If you want someone to stand in the room and watch, I don't mind,' said Yvonne.

'That's very kind of you, Yvonne,' said Maddy. 'The thing is, we need Jess because the library tried to communicate with her, as it did with Luke and me. Your role as support person is just as important, but Jess has to be our witness.'

'Right,' said Yvonne. 'I don't understand, but whatever. Stay put and I'll see what I can do.' She gave Luke the biscuit tin and headed downstairs.

'I wonder what she'll say,' said Luke.

'I don't care, so long as she fetches Jess.' Maddy's fingertips were tingling. She felt as if the room was calling to her.

After a few more minutes, Yvonne's voice echoed round the stairwell. 'I'll be right here, Jess, and I've got biscuits, and I put the mini first-aid kit in my pocket. Not that anyone will need it.'

'Do you promise you'll be outside the door?' Jess's voice had a distinct quiver in it.

'Of course I will. Pinky promise. And you'll be in the room with two experts. They won't let anything happen to you. If you do need me, shout and I'll run in.'

The tops of two heads came into view: Yvonne's blonde curls and Jess's long red hair. 'I still don't like it,' said Jess. 'What if something happens?'

'The thing is,' Yvonne said comfortably, 'nothing really has happened, has it? I mean, nobody's been hurt. Yes, books moved around and people felt some weird stuff, but it could be a lot worse, couldn't it?'

'Hopefully not today,' muttered Luke.

Maddy gave him a surprised glance. 'Are you OK?'

'Kind of.' Luke cracked his knuckles, then leaned over. 'Yvonne can say what she likes, but I've been scared in that room and so have you.'

'I'm not sure I need to hear this right now,' said Maddy. She closed her eyes and tried to think calming thoughts. *The library wants to tell us something. That's all it is. We have to find the right way to listen.*

She remembered their last visit to the reading room with Ludovic, the sudden pull towards the statue of Enriqueta Rylands, the strange sensation as her fingers sank into the marble—

'I know what to do,' she said. 'It may be dangerous.'

'Now you tell me,' said Luke.

'What might be dangerous?' Jess demanded, as she reached the landing.

'It definitely won't be dangerous for you,' said Maddy. 'You can stay right by the reading-room door.'

Jess frowned. 'Inside the room?'

'Yes,' said Maddy. 'I'm hoping it won't take long.'

'I'll make tea for everyone afterwards,' said Yvonne,

and gave the biscuit tin a reassuring rattle.

'Excellent,' said Maddy. 'I suppose we'd better go in.'

Yvonne moved the sign, clicking her tongue as she did. Then she unlocked the door. Maddy reached for the handle, but Yvonne barred her way. 'I'll give you five minutes,' she said. 'When time's up, I'll knock and ask what's going on. If I don't get a reply, I'm coming in. Understood?'

'Understood,' said Maddy. 'Thank you.'

'My pleasure.' Yvonne moved aside, folded her arms and watched them pass in. As the door closed, she called 'Five minutes, and not a second more.'

The reading room was bigger than Maddy remembered, and she experienced the familiar awe as she gazed at the arches, the galleries, the statues. *It's a library*, she told herself. *A place of books. You love books. You know books. What harm can come to you?*

'So what exactly are we doing?' said Jess. She was standing with her back to the door and her hands against it, as if to check it was still there.

Maddy walked halfway up the left-hand aisle, turned and looked at the statue of Enriqueta Rylands. *You're the key to this*, she thought. *You wanted your library to be for everybody. You wouldn't want people to be shut out of this room.*

She felt herself being drawn to the statue. Gently, as if someone had taken her hand and was leading her. 'Luke, I need you to hold my hand.'

'What, now?' said Luke. 'I mean, this is work, sort of.'

'Not like that! Hold on to me.' Maddy held out her left

211

hand, wiggling her fingers, and he grasped it. His palm was slightly damp.

Can I do this? she thought. *Whatever it is…* She glanced at Jess.

What she thinks doesn't matter, she told herself. *You felt something. You felt it more than anyone. If anyone can do this, it's you.*

She swallowed, and walked slowly towards the statue. 'Don't let go,' she said, through gritted teeth.

'I won't,' said Luke. 'Though I still don't understand.'

'I'm not sure I do,' said Maddy. 'Jess!'

Jess jumped. 'Yes, what?'

'If anything . . . happens, and it doesn't look good, go and fetch Yvonne. Don't try to help, just get her.'

Jess's eyes widened. 'OK,' she said.

'I need you to watch what happens.'

'If I leave, I won't—'

'Never mind that now.' The pull was growing stronger. 'You won't let go, Luke?'

'I won't.' His grip tightened. 'Are you speeding up because you want to, or…'

The statue seemed to rush towards her. Maddy put out a hand to save herself and—

Her fingers slipped into a cool, soft substance which offered no resistance, and soon she was up to her wrist, her elbow, her shoulder—

'Maddy!' Luke cried. 'Maddy, stop!' His voice was muffled, as if he was underwater.

'Help!' It was a man's voice, which sounded far away, and fingertips brushed her own.

She opened her mouth to say *Take my hand*, but it was filled with the same cold, yielding sensation. Everything was white, and something cool flowed into her ears. *So pleasant*, she thought. *Clean, refreshing...*

'Maddy!' Luke's voice was even fainter.

An arm wrapped around her waist and pulled at her. *Stop that*, she thought, and wriggled to shake it off.

'Help!' The same voice, louder this time.

I wish people would leave me alone, thought Maddy. *It would be so nice and quiet here, out of all the bother...* Her eyelids fluttered, then closed, but everything was still bright, cool white.

'Maddy! Don't go!'

Her eyes snapped open at the sob in Luke's voice. She saw a faint shape, like the shadow of a hand, and reached out. Her fingers touched a palm, larger than her own. She managed to curl her fingers round the fingertips and pull.

'Thank you,' gasped the voice, and another hand caught her wrist. Then she heard a cross 'Get off me!'

But he's holding me, she thought, confused.

The grip at her waist felt as if it might rip her in two as she was pulled backwards. Her ears popped, and the creaking of the reading-room floor sounded unnaturally loud.

'I thought I'd lost you,' Luke murmured into the back of her neck. His face was wet with tears.

'Someone's holding on to me,' said Maddy.

'Yes, that's me.'

'No, in there.' Her arm was still buried in the statue.

'In there? How?'

213

'Stop asking questions and pull me out!'

With an almighty heave, Luke did just that. He staggered backwards, his arm round Maddy's waist, until they were brought up short by a display case.

'Well,' said Bill. 'I never thought I'd be pleased to see you two, but I really am most grateful.' He settled his glasses on his nose and tugged down the points of his waistcoat. 'I suppose you'll have to go back in, though. For *him*.'

'What the actual…?' said Jess, from the door.

'The silly man was so desperate to get out that I suspect he would have pulled you right in,' Bill said. 'That's why I told him to get off.'

Maddy turned to Luke. 'Can we do this again?'

'I don't mind lending a hand,' said Bill. 'Not that I like the fellow.'

They approached the statue. Luke stood next to it and Bill grasped him round the waist. Finally, Maddy took Luke's hand and carefully reached into the statue.

This time she was barely elbow-deep when a hand caught hers. 'Pull!' she shouted, and was yanked backwards. Someone stumbled, possibly her, and they fell in a heap on the parquet.

'I don't believe we've been formally introduced,' said a voice in her ear. It was a familiar voice, with a strong Mancunian accent. A hand took hers and helped her up. 'I'm Ludovic. Thanks for getting us out of there.'

Maddy studied him. The clothes were identical. So were the glasses and so was the face, but this Ludovic had a good-humoured twinkle in his eye that the impostor completely lacked. 'Pleased to meet you at last,' she said, and shook his hand. 'I'm Maddy, and this is Luke.' She waved a hand at Luke, who was heading over.

'Excuse us a moment,' said Luke, and scooped her into a hug. 'I'm so proud of you,' he murmured into her hair, 'but please don't do that again.'

'That was deeply weird,' said Jess, with a note of reverence in her voice. And when Maddy looked, she was grinning from ear to ear.

CHAPTER 25

Jess peeled herself away from the door and advanced towards Bill and Ludovic. 'Are you definitely real?' she asked, her eyes full of wonder. 'If I touch you, will my hand go straight through?'

'Don't be ridiculous, Jess,' said Bill. 'What do you think we are, ghosts?'

Jess shrugged. 'Maybe. To be honest, Bill, you're hard to get hold of at the best of times, so I wouldn't be surprised.' She turned to Luke and Maddy, an expectant look on her face. 'So, now what?'

'Tea,' Maddy said firmly. 'And maybe a biscuit.' Suddenly, she shivered.

Luke put an arm round her. 'Are you cold?'

'Not exactly.' She rubbed her arms vigorously. 'I don't want to talk about it.'

'It was amazing,' said Jess. 'Wait till I tell Yvonne. She'll be so gutted that she missed it.'

'Right,' said Luke. 'Before anyone leaves this room, you must promise not to tell anyone what just happened.

216

Not until it's the right time.'

'Oh come on,' said Jess. 'Seriously?'

'I shall be making an official complaint,' said Bill. He straightened, then winced. 'This sort of thing can't happen.'

'That's exactly why you must keep quiet,' said Luke. 'We need to catch the person – or persons – who did this, and make sure they can't do it again.'

Bill stared at him. 'Who put you in charge?'

'The Keeper of England, actually,' said Luke. He suspected his expression was smug, but didn't care. 'Maddy and I are in *joint* charge here. So please do as we ask, or you'll have Jemma James to deal with.'

Bill sniffed.

'Not to mention Raphael Burns.'

Bill muttered something and folded his arms.

'I don't know what you're so cross about, Bill,' said Ludovic. 'You were only in there two minutes, comparatively speaking.'

'Yes, with *you*,' said Bill, looking down his nose at him.

'I had to put up with *you*,' said Ludovic. 'It's a two-way street, mate.'

'Can everyone calm down, please,' said Maddy. 'Jess, do you promise not to tell anyone what happened until we give you permission?'

Jess bit her lip and studied the floor.

'Hopefully that won't be very long,' said Maddy. 'To be honest, if you do tell people they won't believe you.'

'Typical,' said Jess, and sighed. 'OK, I promise. But I

saw it, and you know I did.' She beamed at Maddy. 'Especially you. That was so cool! How did you do it?'

'It may have seemed cool,' said Maddy, 'but I was in danger. If I'd gone right into that statue, I might never have come out.'

'Of course you would,' said Luke. 'I'd have found a way to get you out. If there wasn't a way, I'd have gone in there with you. I couldn't leave you there alone.'

Maddy put her hands on his shoulders and gazed into his eyes. 'Would you really have done that for me?'

He nodded. 'I can't imagine life without you.'

Maddy blinked, hard. 'I don't know what to say,' she murmured. She stood on tiptoe, her face upturned to his…

A cough made them look round. 'We are dead grateful and all that,' said Ludovic, 'but someone mentioned tea?'

***

'Where did you two spring from?' said Yvonne, as first Bill, then Ludovic left the reading room.

'Came in through the other entrance,' said Ludovic.

'Why do we even bother putting signs up?' said Yvonne. 'This is a library, can't people read?' She turned to Jess. 'Are you OK?'

Jess grinned. 'More than OK. I'm not allowed to talk about it.' She gave Yvonne a knowing wink.

'Oh,' said Yvonne. 'Does that mean you don't need tea?'

'Oh yeah, definitely tea,' said Jess, with a gleam in her eye. 'And a biscuit. Or two.'

'Reader Services it is,' said Yvonne. 'I'll put up a notice to say we're closed for half an hour and see if anyone pays any attention.'

'I shall go through the reading room and take the lift,' said Bill. 'I'm as stiff as a board.'

'No change there, mate,' said Ludovic, under his breath, and Jess sniggered.

Upstairs, Luke made sure that Maddy drank a whole mug of hot sweet tea and ate a biscuit. She was almost as pale as the statue of Enriqueta Rylands. 'I'm fine,' she said, more than once.

'Just making sure,' he said, and smiled at her.

Jess finished her mug of tea. 'I suppose you want me to make tracks,' she said, and stood up. 'Never saw a thing.'

'Excellent,' said Luke. 'If anyone asks, you had a meeting with us and it came to nothing. Yvonne, the same goes for you.'

'Sorry, what?' said Yvonne, looking up from her phone.

'Luke says thank you for your help,' said Maddy. 'Oh, and we got a message that you're needed in the exhibition galleries.'

'Oh, good,' said Yvonne. 'I like talking to people: it's pretty quiet here.' She stood up. 'If you leave before I get back, do remember to lock the door. And don't eat all my biscuits. They're for emergencies.' She frowned. 'Why are you eating my biscuits?'

'You said we could,' said Luke.

'Did I?'

'Definitely,' Maddy and Ludovic said, together.

Once the two women had gone, Luke took out his notebook and found a fresh page. 'Bill, from what Ludovic says it sounds as if you weren't trapped in the statue for

219

long. Can you tell me how you got there, and what happened beforehand?'

'I can,' said Bill, crossing his legs in a businesslike manner. 'Yesterday I received an email from Mr Wright here, asking for advice.' He jerked a thumb at Ludovic. 'He said he'd noticed on his last visit that the spine of one of the books in the reading room was coming away. I replied that that was impossible, as they are checked regularly, and he invited me to the reading room first thing this morning to see for myself.'

Ludovic shook his head. 'Wasn't me. I was already stuck in the statue.'

'So *you* say,' said Bill, and turned to Luke. 'I came in this morning and went to the reading room. He was already there, waiting. I assumed we'd check the book and I'd take any necessary action, but he started making conversation.' He gave Ludovic a contemptuous glance.

'Where were you standing at this point?' asked Luke.

'In front of the statue. He asked me a question and I was debating how to answer it when he pushed me. I fell backwards, expecting to hit the statue any minute, and instead I sort of fell into it. I shouted for help, obviously, but this man said "You'll be lucky." I have no idea how he did it, but he was right behind me. He was lucky I didn't punch him. I certainly thought about it.'

'Hang on a minute,' said Ludovic. 'I was in the statue the whole time. You can't have met me in the reading room.'

'I hate to say it, Ludovic,' said Maddy, 'but someone has been impersonating you. Possibly for some time.'

220

Ludovic whipped round. 'You what?'

'I'm afraid so,' said Luke. 'We've both met someone who looks exactly like you more than once in the last few days. In the reading room, too. Couldn't you see us?'

'You can't see much when you're trapped inside a statue,' said Ludovic. 'I could sense when people were near, and I could tell the difference between night and day, but that was about it.'

'I agree,' said Maddy. 'When my head was in the statue I could hardly hear you, Luke. And I barely saw Bill's hand, even though he was in there too.'

'So the man I met in the reading room was a fake version of this man,' said Bill. 'A shapeshifter.'

'That's right,' said Luke.

Bill smirked. 'He was very convincing. He was certainly as annoying as the real thing.'

'The morning I spent squashed in that statue with you seemed twice as long as the rest of the time put together,' said Ludovic, with feeling. 'Maybe that's how I finally got Maddy and Luke to figure out where I was and rescue us. The power of exasperation.'

'Can you remember how you ended up in the statue, Ludovic?' asked Luke.

Ludovic's brow furrowed. 'Hmmm . . . that seems a long time ago. I must have been in the reading room for a reason, but what was it? I'm not here that often.'

'Were you meeting somebody?' asked Maddy.

He shrugged. 'I assume so.'

'Doesn't know if he's coming or going,' muttered Bill.

Luke raised his eyebrows and he subsided. 'Maybe

221

you'll remember if you check your calendar,' Luke said, turning to Ludovic. 'Do you have your phone on you?'

'Always got my phone. Not that I could reach it in there…' Ludovic fished it out of his jeans pocket. 'Hang on and I'll do a search.' His thumbs got busy. 'John . . . Rylands.' He hit the magnifying-glass icon and peered at the screen. 'Oh yeah, I remember. Sandy asked me to come over.'

Luke looked up from his notebook. 'Sandy?'

'Yeah, Sandy. Alexander Montague, director of the library. He said he wanted to do a handover before going on sabbatical. I did find it odd that we weren't meeting in his office, but…'

'How did he seem when you met?' asked Maddy.

'Bit odd. Distracted. Normally he's very focused, but he started rambling on that the statues needed restoring. "Touch this," he said, pointing at the one I got stuck in. So I did, and it felt as if I was being sucked through a straw. Horrible.' He shuddered.

'Touch the statue,' murmured Bill, grinning. 'Fancy falling for that.'

'I'm sorry we've made you remember it, Ludovic,' said Maddy. She made to put her hand on his arm, but he flinched away.

Then he frowned. 'Hold up,' he said. 'If someone pretending to be me put Bill in the statue, was the person I met really Sandy?'

'I doubt it,' said Luke. 'I'm wondering if Sandy is actually on sabbatical.'

'If it wasn't Sandy, who was it?'

'We've got a pretty good idea,' said Luke, grimly. 'But there's one way to be absolutely sure.'

Both men looked at him, eyebrows raised. 'Well, go on,' said Ludovic. 'Spit it out.'

'What are you waiting for, man?' said Bill.

Luke glanced at Maddy, who nodded. 'Somehow, we have to lure him to the library and make him show himself.'

CHAPTER 26

Luke and Maddy took the lift with Ludovic, who was checking his phone. 'Fifty-seven missed calls,' he said. 'Two thousand and ten emails.' He heaved a sigh. 'I wish my doppelgänger had taken care of my admin.'

'No chance of that,' said Luke. 'At least you're back in the real world.'

Ludovic managed a wry smile. 'And I thought I was unique.'

The lift pinged and the doors opened. 'I'll go for a walk before I tackle all this.' He waved his phone. 'Appreciate Manchester. And maybe slow down a bit. If I hadn't been rushing from pillar to post, maybe I'd have rumbled what was going on.'

'Don't be too hard on yourself,' said Maddy, as they walked into the foyer.

He winked at her. 'No chance of that. I might stop and smell the flowers more often.'

Soraya stared as Ludovic walked to the desk. 'I didn't see you come in,' she said.

'Maybe I didn't,' he said, with a grin.

'Soraya,' said Luke, 'can you tip us off if Ludovic returns to the library?'

Soraya looked from them to Ludovic. 'Hang on…'

Ludovic headed for the gift shop and beckoned them over. 'I reckon we need a safe word. So you know I'm me, and vice versa.'

'OK,' said Luke, but all that came to mind were obvious words: library, bookshelf, statue…

'Rhino,' said Ludovic.

'All right,' said Maddy. 'Rhino it is.'

'Brill. Catch you later: I'm going for a coffee. Serious caffeine withdrawal.' He raised a hand and walked out.

Luke watched him go. 'His head doesn't bob when he walks,' he said. 'Because his stride isn't as long.'

'It isn't *too* long,' said Maddy. 'His impersonator is obviously a fair bit taller.' Her eyebrows drew together. 'We must put an end to this, and I have no idea how.'

'The first thing to do is leave,' said Luke. 'If the fake Ludovic comes back and sees Gertrude parked outside, he'll twig that something's up.'

'We're not *leaving* leaving, are we?' said Maddy.

'Of course not,' said Luke. 'We'll go to the Airbnb.'

Soraya watched them sign out. 'So… Did you fix the reading room?'

'Partly,' said Luke. 'We need to do a bit more thinking. We'll be in touch. Oh, and if Ludovic asks, we've gone to London.'

'What is this with Ludovic?' said Soraya. 'He can be a bit abrasive, but it's mean to gang up on him—'

'There you are!' Jess dashed towards them. 'It's happening again. In the reading room.'

Soraya rolled her eyes.

Jess led them to the lift, talking all the while. 'I assumed after what happened earlier that the reading room was fine now. So I went in – I've missed it – and I got this weird creepy feeling.'

'OK,' said Luke. 'Did anything happen?'

'I didn't wait to find out,' said Jess. 'I came to find you. I went to Reader Services first, but you weren't there. Then I came here.' The lift doors opened and she ushered them in.

The reading room seemed just as it had when they left. Luke gazed around it. 'Nothing appears wrong,' he said. 'Whereabouts were you, Jess?'

'At the other end,' she said, promptly. 'I felt a sort of tugging. After seeing Maddy go into the statue, I decided I wasn't hanging about.'

'You did the right thing,' said Maddy. She took Luke's hand and together they walked to the far end of the room, where the statue of John Rylands waited for them. 'I'm… I'm a bit tingly. I'm trying to work out if it's real or I'm imagining it.'

'Me too,' said Luke.

Maddy looked at the statue. 'You don't think…'

'It would make sense,' said Luke. 'Why would you trap two people in the same statue if you had a spare one?'

They moved forward until they were within touching distance of the statue. 'It isn't pulling us,' said Maddy.

'Maybe whoever's inside doesn't have strong magical

powers,' said Luke. 'Or any powers.' He grinned. 'I suspect that having Bill in the statue with him made Ludovic work extra hard to attract our attention.'

'You could be right.' Maddy put out a hand, then paused. 'Do you want a go?'

'Me? I can't...'

'You won't know unless you try. I'll hold on to you.'

Luke took a deep breath. *She's right*, he thought. *What if Maddy can do this, and I can't?*

'You can do lots of things that I can't,' said Maddy, as if she had read his thoughts.

He glanced at Jess, who was watching them intently. 'Let's not go into that right now,' he said, and gave Maddy his left hand. 'OK, brace.'

He touched John Rylands' marble knee with the tips of his fore and middle fingers.

Nothing happened.

'Right, that's a no,' he said, stepping back.

'Try again,' said Maddy. 'And try not to think about what you're doing.'

He sighed. 'OK.' He looked away from the statue, so he wouldn't see when his fingers hit the marble...

...and were enveloped by it.

He gasped.

'Jess, hold my other hand,' said Maddy. 'Quickly!'

Luke wondered why she was speaking so quietly as his wrist, then his arm was encased in coolness. A hand grasped his. A large hand, with a rough palm.

'Pull me out!' he shouted. His own voice seemed distant.

227

The slight man who emerged, somehow, from the statue was well dressed in a navy suit with a maroon tie and matching pocket square, and had a head of tousled ash-blond hair which rivalled Raphael's. 'Would you be Sandy Montague?' asked Luke.

'I would,' said the man, with a hint of a Scots accent. 'Who might you be? And how the heck did you do what you just did? I'd given up hope.'

'It's a long story,' said Luke. 'Can I ask… When this happened to you, had you been asked to meet someone in this reading room?'

Sandy Montague looked at him with piercing blue eyes. 'I had,' he said. 'I came in specially, because he's a rare visitor. The person I met with was Raphael Burns.'

***

'I thought conducting an investigation would make things clearer,' said Luke. 'Not more complicated.'

They were sitting on the sofa in their apartment, reading. Gertrude hunkered outside the window.

'Maybe it's like tidying a bookshelf,' said Maddy. 'Maybe we're at the point where it gets worse before it gets better.'

'I hope so,' said Luke. He scowled at his book. 'I wish this was easier to read.' He'd expected a book on transformation to be exciting, but the sentences were long and convoluted.

'Is there an index?' said Maddy.

Luke flicked to the back of the book. 'Oh yeah.' He ran a finger down the columns, seeking a shortcut… 'Wait a minute. Where did we put those Pencils of Truth?'

Maddy looked up from her book. 'They're still in Gertrude.'

'Right.' Luke sprang up, got Gertrude's keys and went outside. Two minutes later he returned, holding the pencils aloft like a flaming torch. 'If this works...' He gave a pencil to Maddy, opened his book at a page near the end, closed his eyes and brought the pencil down.

He opened his eyes.

Detection, danger of ...... 220.

'Yes!' he cried, and riffled through the pages. 'Here we are.' He scanned the page. 'Listen to this, Maddy. *Unsurprisingly, the greatest risk of detection lies in those who are intimately acquainted either with you or the person whom you purport to be. Those who know you may glimpse one of your distinctive mannerisms or tricks of speech beneath the veneer you have adopted. Those who know your alter ego will pick up on any discrepancies. Equally, your most successful transformation will always be into someone you know well. Your best chance of success is a short impersonation of that person, conducted in front of people for whom they are a comparative stranger.*'

'I think I've got that,' said Maddy.

'Basically, whoever's inside fake Ludovic may not know him that well, but they don't need to,' said Luke. 'He's always flitting from meeting to meeting, so they don't have to sustain the pretence for long.'

'How are we going to unmask him?' said Maddy. 'We already know he isn't Ludovic, but how do we prove it?'

'We could produce the real Ludovic,' said Luke, 'if he's

up for it. Or… Is there anything in your book that would help?'

'If Lennox did write this book, he's even more horrid than I thought,' said Maddy. 'That's saying something.' She closed her eyes, opened the book at random and carefully brought her pencil's tip to the page. 'Here's what the pencil has found.' She read aloud. '*I shall never forget that night in Rome. I slipped away from the consul's reception with a small morocco-bound volume nestled in the inside pocket of my coat. A small item, but priceless. I knew I would love that volume more than a consul ever could. Therefore, by right, it belonged to me. It was my first theft – my first, exhilarating theft – and it would not be my last.*'

'A book thief,' said Luke, and his lip curled.

'If we confront him with that,' said Maddy, 'it might shake his identity.'

'Assuming it is Lennox in there, not Brian,' said Luke.

'I worked with Brian for years and years,' said Maddy. 'I can imagine him doing one transformation for a short while to get something, but a string of them? That's much more like Lennox.'

'I agree,' said Luke. 'But… These transformations have given this person access to multiple libraries full of valuable books. How do we know he hasn't been stealing them?'

Maddy stared at him. 'We don't,' she said. 'What I do know is that we need help.'

Luke met her eyes. 'You're right, Maddy. This is too big for us to handle on our own. I'll phone Jemma.'

Jemma answered on the first ring. 'Are you both all right?' she said. 'I've been worried sick.'

'We're both fine,' said Luke. 'I have a report to make.'

As he spoke, Jemma gasped. 'You're kidding me,' she said. 'I'm not standing for this. I'll arrange cover and get on the next train. You two can stand down.'

'No!' cried Maddy. 'That's what he wants.'

Luke looked over. She was trembling like a leaf about to fall.

'I guarantee that he doesn't,' said Jemma.

'Think, Jemma. He's tricked a whole series of people, including an Assistant Keeper, and trapped them. How do you know he isn't planning to do that to you? To take your place?'

A long pause. 'So what do we do?' asked Jemma. 'We can't do nothing.'

'I agree,' said Luke. 'But we need to be very, *very* careful.'

CHAPTER 27

Luke checked the time. 'He's due any minute.' He glanced at Maddy who, in the form of Yvonne, was tidying the display of pen nibs in the gift shop. 'I can't get used to it.'

Maddy looked round and grinned. 'It's only temporary,' she said, out of the side of her mouth. 'Stand straight. Josh doesn't slouch like that.'

Luke drew himself up. 'I have no idea how anyone can do this for any length of time,' he said. 'It's exhausting.'

'I imagine it's easier when you get used to it,' said Maddy. 'I have a terrible urge to make tea.'

'I can't think why,' said Luke. 'Anyway, you'll have to wait till afterwards. We'll probably need it. And a biscuit.'

Across the foyer, Soraya coughed.

'Here we go,' said Luke.

Ludovic swaggered in – or rather, the person pretending to be Ludovic. They had already seen the real thing an hour earlier.

'Good morning, Ludovic,' said Soraya. 'Are you here for the meeting?'

'Oh yes. Nice of Jemma to come all this way just to say thank you to little old me. Shame she couldn't be bothered to lend a hand, mind.'

Luke saw Maddy's hand clench and moved to her side. 'Don't let him get to you,' he whispered.

'Jemma's already gone to the reading room,' said Soraya.

'I'll make tracks, then,' said the fake Ludovic. 'She hinted in her email that she was planning a bit of restructuring up north. Let's see if I'm an Assistant Keeper when I come down, eh?'

'Careful,' murmured Maddy.

Luke uncurled his own fists. 'I'll be so glad when this is over,' he whispered.

He moved forward as the man headed towards the stairwell. *Lift or stairs?* he thought.

His target seemed to have the same question in mind. Then he grinned and began to climb the stairs, looking about him.

Luke ran to the lift and thumped the call button. Maddy was close behind. They dashed in as soon as the doors opened.

'I want to hug you,' said Luke, 'but I can't.'

'You absolutely can't,' said Maddy. 'That might break the transformation. We may not need it much longer, but we can't risk it.'

The lift moved slowly upward. *Who will get there first?* thought Luke.

They forced themselves to walk out of the lift in a dignified manner. Jess was waiting in the anteroom, and gave them both a thumbs up and a huge grin.

Luke opened the reading-room door and peeped round it.

Hermione Dawes was standing in the centre of the room, dressed in a grey trouser suit and a bright pink top which matched the beads at her throat. A pink handbag was on the floor beside her. 'Is that…'

'Rhino,' said Luke.

'Yes, rhino,' said Maddy.

Hermione smiled. 'Good to know. I take it he's on his way. Got your pencils?'

Luke's hand went to his pocket. He saw Maddy do the same.

'Hello, Ludovic,' said Jess, loudly.

Luke and Maddy hurried down the aisle and took up position near Hermione.

The door opened. 'Well, hello th—' The fake Ludovic stopped dead. 'Where's Jemma?' he asked.

'I'm afraid she couldn't make it,' said Hermione, blandly. 'She was called to a book emergency this morning, so she asked me to deputise. Hermione Dawes, Assistant Keeper.' She put out her hand, and Luke realised she was wearing white gloves.

The man strode over, head bobbing. 'Charmed, I'm sure,' he said, as they shook hands. 'Almost as good as the real thing. Now, shall we talk business? Jemma said she was looking to shake things up a bit. Why don't we take a walk, and you can tell me what she's got in mind.'

Hermione didn't move a step. 'I wish I could,' she said. 'Unfortunately, Jemma didn't have time to brief me thoroughly before she left. She'll schedule a video call with you instead.'

'Fair enough. From the horse's mouth, and all that.' He stood his ground, hands clasped behind his back, rocking slightly on the balls of his feet.

'What Jemma has authorised is a bonus payment, in recognition of your prompt and valuable assistance.' Hermione took a thick envelope, a form and a Pencil of Truth from her bag. 'So if you'll sign as proof of receipt...' She put the form and the pencil on the nearest table.

He frowned. 'Surely pen would be more appropriate.'

'Pencil is fine,' said Hermione. 'I'll trust you.'

The man in Ludovic's form sat down, picked up the pencil, twirled it in his right hand and brought it to the paper.

The lead broke on the downstroke of the L.

He looked up. 'This is why we use pens.'

Luke stepped forward. 'Try mine,' he said, holding the pencil at arm's length.

The other man grabbed it. 'Ta.'

The point broke on contact with the paper.

'We have a problem,' said Hermione. 'Any idea why?'

'I have,' said a voice behind them.

The door of the periodical room opened and Ludovic came out, his thumbs in the belt loops of his jeans. 'This chancer stole my identity and imprisoned me in there.' He pointed to the statue of Enriqueta Rylands, who gazed on impassively.

The other Ludovic appeared completely unfazed. 'You mean *you've* stolen *my* identity.'

'What's the safe word?' said Ludovic, folding his arms.

'Safe word? What on earth are you talking about? What rubbish is this?' He lunged for the envelope, but Hermione moved it away. 'And who says he's real?'

'I do.'

This time the voice came from the other end of the room, and Bill came out of the door marked *Librarian*. 'You imprisoned me, too, with him. You pushed me. You laid hands on me.' He stalked forward, fists clenching and unclenching.

'Curiouser and curiouser,' remarked Hermione.

The man unleashed a charming smile which looked completely wrong on Ludovic's face. 'There must be a misunderstanding. I would never push anyone.' He put down the Pencil of Truth and raised his hands as if in surrender. 'Are these the hands of a violent man?'

Bill was still advancing doggedly, like a charge in exceedingly slow motion. 'We know very well you're not him,' he said. 'So who are you?'

Maddy stepped forward, taking a Pencil of Truth from her pocket. She grabbed the false Ludovic's hand and pushed the point of the pencil into his palm. 'Let's find out.'

It was astonishing to watch. The skin of both seemed to ripple. Yvonne's form shrank, while Ludovic grew taller and broader. Yvonne's blonde hair uncurled, lengthened and grew dark, while Ludovic's glasses vanished and his shoulders strained the seams of his black T-shirt, which transformed into a crisp white shirt under a beautifully-cut navy suit. A moment later, the sea-green eyes of Lennox

Nash glared at them. But the shiny bald head of Ludovic remained.

'Thought so,' said Maddy, pocketing the pencil.

'So I played a little prank,' said Lennox. 'You can't prove a thing. It's this man's word against mine.'

'And mine,' said Bill. 'I've heard of you, but I never thought I'd meet you in the flesh.' He looked Lennox up and down. 'They say it's a mistake to meet your idols, and they're absolutely right.'

A door creaked open at the end of the room. 'What's in there?' murmured Luke.

'Fire apparatus,' said Maddy. 'And Sandy Montague.'

'I trust my word counts for something, too,' said Sandy. 'I've lost six weeks of my sabbatical, thanks to you. My publisher will be furious. I fully intend to press charges.'

'For what?' said Lennox. 'We haven't met in years.'

'Not in your current form,' said Sandy. 'But I remember you very well. Although last time I saw you, you had hair.'

Lennox Nash reached up, ran his hand over his head and uttered an anguished cry.

'What have we got so far?' said Hermione. 'Impersonation, identity theft, fraud, false imprisonment, assault, maybe actual theft...' She counted on her gloved fingers.

'I don't have to stand here and listen to this twaddle.' Lennox turned and made for the door.

'Oh yes you do,' muttered Maddy. She ran to the nearest bookcase and placed her hands on the glass, then jumped back as the doors swung open and books flew out. Not just from that bookcase: from all the bookcases.

237

Books hurtled towards Lennox, barring his way, and began building a tight circular wall around him. He tried to beat them off, but they dodged him. The wall grew higher and higher until a neat pillar of books finished in a dome echoing the curve of his round bald head. The only sign of Lennox's presence was the occasional muffled cry.

A team of police officers burst in. 'Where's the escapee?' asked the sergeant, a stocky dark-haired man with a neat beard.

They pointed to the pillar of books.

The police officer approached it. 'Is that you, Lennox Nash?'

Silence. Then a small voice said, 'Um, yes.'

'This is Sergeant Jefferson speaking, of the Greater Manchester Police. Will you come quietly?'

'Yes, sir.'

'Good.' The sergeant turned. 'Unpack him, officers. We'll cuff him, just in case. Though this slippery customer will be going to a much more secure facility than the previous one.'

Hermione walked up. 'There'll be several additional charges to add to the list, Sergeant Jefferson,' she said. 'You can get the details from these two. I imagine that will come much later.'

'All in good time, madam,' said the sergeant. 'Come on, look lively,' he said to the officers carefully dismantling the tower of books, supervised by Bill. 'We haven't got all day.' He pulled a set of handcuffs from a pouch on his belt and moved forward.

Luke sidled over to Maddy. 'Am I still in Josh's form?'

he asked.

She gave him a slow, sweet smile. 'No, you're you. You changed back at the same time as I did.'

'Excellent.' He reached out, then stopped. 'You aren't going to unleash anything else, are you?'

'I'm not planning to,' said Maddy, and stepped into his embrace. Someone whistled – he rather thought it was Ludovic – and the sun streamed through the stained-glass window, bathing them in gentle, multicoloured light.

CHAPTER 28

A bolt of lightning split the sky outside Severndroog Castle as Em pinned Maddy's veil in place. 'I hope this tower has got a lightning rod,' she muttered.

'You're not scared, are you?' said Maddy, craning to peer through the window. 'This is great! I couldn't have asked for better weather.'

'I'm glad you're happy,' said Em, rather nervously.

'Oh yes,' said Maddy. 'It'll be even better when we're upstairs. If it doesn't rain, perhaps we can have our wedding photos on the roof after all.'

She gazed out again. Beyond the trees, London was spread around them like an extremely complicated quilt. Then she regarded herself in the mirror. 'Do I look pale?'

'You're getting married in a Gothic folly in the woods in the middle of a thunderstorm,' said Em. 'It would hardly do to be pink-cheeked and bursting with health, would it?'

'I suppose,' said Maddy.

'You'll probably go pink when you see Luke, anyway.'

Maddy giggled. 'Why, what is he wearing?' Her smile

faded. 'What *is* he wearing?'

'It's all under control,' said Em, which didn't reassure Maddy in the slightest. 'Don't worry: he hasn't borrowed anything from Raphael.'

Something borrowed… Maddy checked her wedding inventory. *My engagement ring is an antique: that's something old. My dress is new.* She lifted her skirt and felt for her blue ribbon garter. 'Something borrowed…'

Em took a deep purple rose from the vase on the side table and carefully inserted it in Maddy's bouquet. 'I doubt the venue will mind. Oh, and you're borrowing Luna.'

'So I am.' Luna was conducting a pre-event wash beneath one of the chairs, while Folio attended to the kittens. 'Will Folio mind kitten-sitting?'

Em shrugged. 'They're his kittens. I wouldn't have had him down for a stay-at-home dad, but there you go.' She checked her watch. 'Look at the time! If you're going to nail your entrance, we'd better get moving.'

Maddy caught up her bouquet and headed for the door. 'Come on, Luna!'

She had thought hard about the question of bridesmaids. She could have asked several people: Em, Jemma, even Hermione Dawes, who had helped her and Luke in a time of need. She also had distant family who might make the effort to come. Jemma was already Luke's best woman, though. And with just a few weeks before their wedding date, not to mention plenty of other things to think about, she had decided to keep things simple. The beauty of having a black cat as her attendant was that Luna didn't require dresses or accessories.

241

Maddy ascended the stairs, holding her skirts out of the way. Raphael was waiting at the entrance to the room where the wedding would take place. For a wonder, he was most suitably attired in a morning suit and top hat. His black tie was spangled with silver stars, but Maddy felt that was entirely permissible.

'Is Luke in there?' said Maddy, breathlessly.

Raphael smiled. 'He's been in there twitching for the last twenty minutes,' he said. 'I'd say I've got the easy job today, compared to Jemma.' He offered an arm. 'You look amazing, Maddy.'

'Why, thank you,' Maddy replied. She couldn't keep the grin off her face.

Em bustled forward and arranged Maddy's veil. 'Nearly time,' she murmured.

There was a crack outside, followed by a stentorian rumble.

'Wow,' said Raphael. 'I felt that.'

'I'm taking it as a good omen,' said Maddy.

Above them, a bell tolled.

'Bang on the hour,' said Raphael, and threw open the door.

A roomful of guests turned to stare. There were gasps, cheers, applause. Several people took a photo.

Raphael walked forward slowly with Maddy on his arm. It was almost like being back in her dream, except that the guests were sitting on chairs and Raphael was beside her, while the registrar, in a neat grey skirt suit, waited at the front. On the right was Luke, who was gaping at her as if he had never seen her before. He was in black and midnight blue, just like her dream, but even handsomer than his dream version. Next to him was Jemma, blooming in an indigo Empire-line dress sprinkled with white moonflowers.

As she walked, in her peripheral vision Maddy glimpsed the guests: fellow Gothic-literature fans, the Golden Age ladies, Mohammed, Susie her yoga teacher and friends from the class, Jasper Bantam, Hermione, Giulia, Carl. There were new faces, too: Jess, Soraya, Yvonne, Josh, Ludovic, and sitting in another row, Bill. Sandy Montague was there too, as dapper as Raphael.

At last Maddy reached the front of the room. She turned to Luke and slowly raised her veil. He took her hands and gazed into her eyes.

The registrar coughed.

Luke took no notice. Still gazing at Maddy, he tucked a stray curl behind her ear. 'You're so beautiful,' he murmured.

'Aaaahh,' breathed the guests.

The registrar coughed again and Maddy and Luke hastily faced her. 'Ladies and gentlemen…'

After the ceremony, the rain stopped for long enough to allow a few photos on the castle's rooftop viewing platform. First, the happy couple posed for solo pictures.

'Can I ask you something?' murmured Maddy, as the photographer fussed with his camera.

'You can ask me anything,' said Luke, grinning.

'Are you…' He leaned in, and it was all she could do not to kiss him. 'Are you using glamour?' she asked suspiciously.

He laughed. 'No! This must be what I look like when I'm ridiculously happy.' He gazed at her searchingly. 'Are you, though?'

She grinned and gave him a playful tap on the arm. 'I wouldn't know how!' And the photographer snapped a photo of them sharing the joke.

'Maybe it's related to being sort of immortal,' she said later, as their guests, dressed in all colours as instructed, arranged themselves around them.

'In that case, I shall enjoy being even handsomer than usual for the foreseeable future,' said Luke, smugly.

Maddy rolled her eyes. 'Don't make me regret this.'

'Everyone!' called the photographer. 'Say cheese.'

'Cheese!' chorused most people, with occasional shouts of 'Camembert!', 'Mascarpone!' and 'Brie!'

'I hope no uninvited guests turn up at the reception,' muttered Maddy, as the photographer arranged the next shot.

'There's no chance of that,' said Luke. 'The room will be absolutely full of members of the Keepers' Guild, and no one can get in without a password. Besides, Sergeant Hawkins is on security. I'd like to see anyone try to get past him.'

'True,' said Maddy. 'So I just have to worry about the food and Ludovic's taste in music. It was kind of him to offer to DJ as a wedding present, but…'

'Trust me,' said Luke, putting his arms around her, 'it's all in hand. You don't have to worry about a thing.'

The borscht was beautifully seasoned, the cauliflower steak perfectly cooked, the roast beef utterly succulent, the blood orange and raspberry sorbets zingy and refreshing. Goblets of ruby wine were raised to the bride and groom. Even the speeches were touching, amusing and mercifully short.

The guests sipped champagne and mocktails as Ludovic set up his equipment. Maddy wondered whether his gold lamé dinner jacket and matching cap had been acquired for the occasion, or were what Ludovic considered normal evening wear.

'Right, folks,' he announced. 'Let's dim those lights and call on the bride and groom for their first dance. I give you . . . Luke Varney and Maddy Shenton!'

Among the applause, Luke led Maddy to the floor. Maddy could hear the guests whispering to each other. And as the first notes of the Goo Goo Dolls' 'Iris' rang out, everything but Luke faded away as she circled in his arms, safe and happy.

Safe, for now. Lennox Nash is back under guard, in a secure prison, but he's still capable of using his charm. While his powers were curtailed and his membership of the Keepers' Guild suspended, somehow he's acquired new abilities. Possibly even some that he didn't have before. And we don't know where Brian is. Or any missing books...

'You're thinking, aren't you,' said Luke, in her ear.

'Sorry,' said Maddy. 'It's difficult not to. But at least we've managed to get married, and you're a legal person.'

'Yes,' said Luke. 'And Jemma has extended our Associate Keeper roles for the next six months, at least.'

Maddy giggled. 'Aren't we important?' Then they

245

realised that while they were circling the floor, the music had stopped. They laughed and shared a kiss, then invited everyone to dance.

'You don't think Jemma extending my promotion was just a wedding present, do you?' she murmured, as they watched Raphael, Carl, Ludovic and Jess pogoing to 'She Sells Sanctuary.'

'Don't be daft,' said Luke. 'We solved a massive case and sorted out Lennox Nash with minimal help. If anything, you deserve the promotion more than I do. You're . . . not a different person, but a more powerful person, because you've found your magic. You rescued Bill and Ludovic, and got me to rescue Sandy. And what you did to trap Lennox…' He grinned. 'I'll make sure to stay on your good side.'

'Now who's being daft.'

'Besides, Jemma is more than happy to live the quiet life in the shop for a while. As is Raphael. Now we've finally got a capable Assistant Keeper in post' – he indicated Hermione, who was chatting with Jemma, her pink beads fashioned into a choker for the occasion – 'we can take a breather from the case for a few days and go on honeymoon.'

She looked up at him. 'Still Whitby?'

He squeezed her hand. 'Still Whitby.'

'With a quick diversion to Manchester?'

'Oh yes.' The corner of his mouth crept up. 'Pack your wedding dress.'

She put a hand on his arm. 'Why?'

'Because I've arranged a photoshoot for us at the

library. I know you wanted photos there, and I'm not going to be left out.'

Maddy squealed and held him tight. 'I never thought I could be so happy!'

'Hopefully this is just the beginning,' said Luke, though his voice was muffled. He extricated himself gently and winked at her. 'And now, let's boogie.'

WHAT TO READ NEXT

I've assumed that many of this book's readers will have found it via the Magical Bookshop series. If you haven't, that's my next recommendation, so that you can find out where it all began!

When Jemma James takes a job at Burns Books, the second-worst secondhand bookshop in London, she finds her ambition to turn it around thwarted at every step. Raphael, the owner, is more interested in his newspaper than sales. Folio the bookshop cat has it in for Jemma, and the shop itself appears to have a mind of its own. Or is it more than that?

The first in the series, *Every Trick in the Book*, is here: http://mybook.to/bookshop1.

If you've enjoyed the magic and you fancy a lighter fantasy read, why not try the Lulmouth Bay series which I write with Paula Harmon?

Welcome to Lulmouth Bay, a seaside town with a difference. It's a magical town where imps, elves, Enchanters and merpeople mix with normal folk, and romance may be just around the corner...

The first book in the series is *A Tale of Tea and Dragons*, and you can find it here: http://mybook.to/LBay1.

Finally, if you'd like a shorter read, meet The Spirit of the Law! In this novella series, a modern-day police constable and a hundred-year-old ghost team up to solve the coldest of cases.

The first book is *The Case of the Four Fingers* and you can see it here: http://mybook.to/Fingers.

ACKNOWLEDGEMENTS

As ever, my first thanks go to my beta readers, Carol Bissett, Ruth Cunliffe and Stephen Lenhardt, who whipped through this book. Particular thanks go to Paula Harmon, who alpha read the novel to make sure I hadn't gone too far down the rabbit hole of spinoffs!

Thanks also to my meticulous and speedy proofreader, John Croall, who has declared the book howler-free – always a relief!

For once, I actually live quite near the setting of this novel, so I spent a happy day double-checking the layout of the library and casing various coffee shops to see whether they'd be suitable for Luke! The coffee shops are real, as is Namaste Nepal, and I can confirm that the dil-khush masala is every bit as delicious as Luke found it – and huge! Oh yes, and Severndroog Castle is a real Gothic folly in London.

The John Rylands Library is also real, and equally impressive in real life. However, all the staff I have depicted are fictional, and I'm pretty sure that however magical the library looks, it actually isn't (sorry).

And finally, many thanks to you, dear reader! I hope you've enjoyed this book. If you have, please consider leaving a short review or a rating on Amazon and/or Goodreads. Reviews and ratings are very important to authors, as they help books to find new readers.

FONT AND IMAGE CREDITS

Fonts:

Main title lettering: hand-drawn by me and edited in Procreate and GIMP. Not to be used without permission.

Series, author and chapter heading font: Cinzel/Cinzel Decorative by Natanael Gama: https://www.fontsquirrel.com/fonts/cinzel. License — SIL Open Font License v.1.10: http://scripts.sil.org/OFL.

Graphics:

Book and sparks/fire: by tomert at Depositphotos.
Map of Manchester (recoloured): OpenFreeMap https://openfreemap.org/ © OpenMapTiles https://www.openmaptiles.org/ Data from OpenStreetMap https://www.openstreetmap.org/copyright (licensed via https://creativecommons.org/licenses/by-sa/2.0/). Many thanks to Zsolt Ero for confirming I could use the map!
Cover created using GIMP image editor: www.gimp.org

ABOUT LIZ HEDGECOCK

Liz Hedgecock grew up in London, England, did an English degree, and then took forever to start writing. After several years working in the National Health Service, some short stories crept into the world. A few even won prizes. Then the stories started to grow longer…

Now Liz travels between the nineteenth and twenty-first centuries, murdering people. To be fair, she does usually clean up after herself.

Liz's reimaginings of Sherlock Holmes and her Victorian and contemporary mystery series (two written with Paula Harmon) are available in ebook and paperback.

Liz lives in Cheshire with her husband and two sons, and when she's not writing you can usually find her reading, painting, messing about on social media, or cooing over stuff in museums and art galleries. That's her story, anyway, and she's sticking to it.

Website/blog: http://lizhedgecock.wordpress.com
Facebook: http://www.facebook.com/lizhedgecockwrites
Bluesky: https://bsky.app/profile/lizhedgecock.bsky.social
Instagram: https://www.instagram.com/lizhedgecock/
Goodreads: https://www.goodreads.com/lizhedgecock

BOOKS BY LIZ HEDGECOCK

To check out any of my books, please visit my Amazon author page at http://author.to/LizH. If you follow me there, you'll be notified whenever I release a new book.

The Magical Bookshop (6 novels)
An eccentric owner, a hostile cat, and a bookshop with a mind of its own. Can Jemma turn around the second-worst secondhand bookshop in London? And can she learn its secrets?

Lulmouth Bay (2 novels, with Paula Harmon)
Welcome to Lulmouth Bay, a seaside town with a difference. It's a magical town where imps, elves, Enchanters and merpeople mix with normal folk and romance may be just around the corner…

Booker & Fitch Mysteries (6 novels, with Paula Harmon)
Jade Fitch hopes for a fresh start when she opens a new-age shop in a picturesque market town. Meanwhile, Fi Booker runs a floating bookshop as well as dealing with her teenage son. And as soon as they meet, it's murder…

Maisie Frobisher Mysteries (6 novels)
When Maisie Frobisher, a bored young Victorian socialite, goes travelling in search of adventure, she finds more than she could ever have dreamt of. Mystery, intrigue and a touch of romance.

Caster & Fleet Mysteries (6 novels, with Paula Harmon)
There's a new detective duo in Victorian London . . . and they're women! Meet Katherine and Connie, two young women who become partners in crime. Solving it, that is!

Mrs Hudson & Sherlock Holmes (3 novels)
Mrs Hudson is Sherlock Holmes's elderly landlady. Or is she? Find out her real story here.

Pippa Parker Mysteries (6 novels)
Meet Pippa Parker: mum, amateur sleuth, and resident of a quaint English village called Much Gadding. And then the murders began…

The Spirit of the Law (3 novellas)
Meet a detective duo – a century apart! A modern-day police constable and a hundred-year-old ghost team up to solve the coldest of cases.

Sherlock & Jack (3 novellas)
Jack has been ducking and diving all her life. But when she meets the great detective Sherlock Holmes they form an unlikely partnership. And Jack discovers that she is more important than she ever realised…

Tales of Meadley (3 novelettes)
A romantic comedy mini-series based in the village of Meadley, with a touch of mystery too.

Halloween Sherlock (3 noveletes)

Short dark tales of Sherlock Holmes and Dr Watson, perfect for a grim winter's night.

For children

A Christmas Carrot (with Zoe Harmon)
Perkins the Halloween Cat (with Lucy Shaw)
Rich Girl, Poor Girl (for 9-12 year olds)

WHITE
RHINO
BOOKS

Printed in Dunstable, United Kingdom